Ever After

A Cinderella Story

Ever After

A Cinderella Story

BY WENDY LOGGIA

BASED ON THE SCREENPLAY
BY SUSANNAH GRANT
AND ANDY TENNANT
& RICK PARKS

Dell

Published by
Bantam Doubleday Dell Books for Young Readers
a division of
Bantam Doubleday Dell Publishing Group, Inc.
1540 Broadway
New York, New York 10036

The trademark Laurel-Leaf Library® is registered in the U.S. Patent and Trademark Office.

The trademark Dell® is registered in the U.S. Patent and Trademark Office.

ISBN: 0-440-22815-8

Printed in the United States of America
September 1998
OPM   10   9   8   7   6

Prologue
1500

Long walks in the moonlight, unexpected tokens of affection, a gallant young prince on a majestic horse . . . what girl hasn't dreamed of being swept off her feet by love in a fairy-tale romance?

Once upon a time, in the captivating French countryside, a girl named Danielle dreamed that very dream.

But she did so only after her other dreams had been shattered. . . .

⁓

The early-morning sun had barely risen over the shingled roof of the Manoir de Barbarac when eight-year-old Danielle de Barbarac let out a cry of pure joy.

"Christmas! I get a mother and sisters all on one day!" Danielle's brown eyes sparkled as she smiled up into the dimpled faces of her middle-aged chambermaids, Paulette and Louise. They were doing their best to get her dressed and groomed for what was sure to be a very extraordinary day.

Paulette sucked in her cheeks and tried to look stern. "Yes, it should be very exciting around here, what with a baroness and all." She grasped Danielle's tiny shoulders with firm yet compassionate hands as she wrestled some imaginary wrinkles from the girl's bodice. "Now, hold still."

Danielle complied, her gaze drifting to the gilded mirror that hung on her bedroom wall. At the sight of her reflection, she let out a small gasp. She looked so . . . so different! Where were the knots in her hair? The smudges of dirt on her cheeks? The telltale traces of tree climbing and stream jumping on the hem of her skirts? Gone too was the earthy meadow scent on her skin.

Instead, the vision of a beautiful girl, dressed in pale pink silk and lace, with her sweet-smelling hair up in shell combs, stared back at her.

She felt like a princess.

Danielle couldn't wait to show this new and improved version of herself to her father. He would be so pleased to see her looking so unlike her usual unkempt self.

"The master deserves some happiness after all this time," Louise said, interrupting Danielle's thoughts. "She must be lovely."

"She" was Danielle's new stepmother, the baroness Rodmilla de Ghent. Danielle was to meet her for the very first time that day.

A tiny trickle of sweat slid down Danielle's back as Louise fluffed and straightened her skirt. "I hope she likes me," Danielle said in a small voice.

Louise chucked her under the chin. "She will love you. Just be the little angel I know is in there someplace."

"And don't go chewing on the bones at dinner and give yourself away," Paulette admonished, giving Danielle's hair one last brushing.

Danielle giggled. Her table manners left a little to be desired, but she could be quite a lady when she wanted to be.

And she wanted to be a lady that day . . . more than anything.

Just then a scattering of tiny stones hit the bedroom window. Pulling away from her chambermaids' fussing hands, Danielle hurried to the window and flung it open.

"Gustave, I told you, not today!" she shouted down.

On the ground below stood a scrawny peasant boy, dressed in faded work pants and a soft cotton shirt. As usual, his hair stuck out in unsightly clumps, and his cheeks were sunburned from long days spent roaming the fields and the banks of the Loire.

Gustave gaped up at her. "You look like a *girl!*" he exclaimed, as if by looking that way she had somehow betrayed him.

She shook her head, exasperated. "That's what I am, half-wit!"

"Aye!" he said. "But today you look it!" Danielle watched as Gustave paraded back and forth on the dirt path below her window. He fluffed his hair and lifted his nose so high in the air he almost toppled over. Danielle frowned at his impersonation. She might *look* like a girl, but there was no way she was going to act like *that.*

And there was no way she was going to stand there and let Gustave mock her. "Boy or girl, I can still whip you," she hollered. She turned on her heel and tore out of the room before Paulette or Louise could catch her.

Her shiny new boots flew down the steps at lighting speed. In seconds she had raced through the drawing room and burst out the front door, bent on showing Gustave no mercy.

She let out a whoop and raced after her best friend, his laughter only firing her up more. Dirt flew up in tiny tornadoes as the two children ran around the yard. Paulette and Louise followed, giving halfhearted middle-aged chase.

Danielle was so caught up in her pursuit of Gustave that she failed to see her father's head steward, Maurice, in full dress uniform, as well as the Manoir de Barbarac's staff of fifteen, standing nervously in line at the manor's entrance. But she couldn't miss the urgency in Maurice's voice when he called out to her.

"Danielle! Quickly, girl. It's your father!"

But there was no time. Before she could draw a much-needed breath or notice the mess the chase had made of her appearance, a caravan of coaches had entered the front gate, thundering hooves pounding the dusty driveway. At the lead rode an attractive man on a black stallion, a dark velvet cape billowing behind him.

"Papa," whispered Danielle, her heart racing at the sight.

Maurice bowed slightly as the stallion stopped before him. "Welcome home, *monsieur le seigneur*. I see you have brought us a baroness."

Auguste de Barbarac swung off the horse in a fluid, effortless move. "I have brought you an entire household, Maurice." He scanned the line. "But I seem to be missing a daughter."

The coaches had dropped back—all except

one, the most elaborate. It pulled up in front of the manor, and two coachmen leaped to open the door. Everyone—especially Danielle—held their breath as a tall, elegantly dressed woman stepped out of the carriage. Two girls who appeared to be Danielle's age followed.

The woman was what Danielle would call handsome, not beautiful. She was wearing a burgundy-colored dress, and her glossy black hair was pulled back into a tight, elaborately styled bun. High, angular cheekbones took up much of her face, and her thin lips were painted a deep crimson. Her narrow eyes scanned the house, the yard, the line of eager, nervous servants. Her Roman nose wrinkled involuntarily with the slightest show of displeasure, as if she had smelled rotting meat. But then the wrinkle was gone, and she turned to Danielle's father with a radiant smile.

"Oh, Auguste, it is absolutely charming. Really." She took his arm. "And where is the main house?"

"Papa!" Danielle cried, tossing decorum to the wind. Her excitement bubbled over, and she raced toward her father, throwing her arms around him in a bear hug.

Auguste lifted her in the air and squeezed her with all his might. "Look at you!" he said, laughing as they pulled apart. He took in the mud on his daughter's skirt, the dust on her cheeks, and her now tangled hair. "Well," he laughed, "you're just as I left. And I wager your friend Gustave is around here someplace."

Danielle drew her finger across her neck. "No, sir. I slaughtered him!"

A movement at the side of the house caught their eyes, and father and daughter turned to see Gustave, a human mud pie, as he shuffled toward them, his head hung low.

Auguste's lips curled into a smile. "So you did." He bent toward her ear and whispered, "I had hoped to present a little lady . . . but I guess you will have to do." He set Danielle gently down on the ground and kissed the top of her head.

Danielle swallowed hard as she turned to face the baroness and her daughters.

"Danielle," her father said, "may I present the baroness Rodmilla de Ghent and her daughters, Marguerite and Jacqueline?"

Danielle bent her small form into her best curtsy, praying that she didn't shake too much. *"Madame, mesdemoiselles,"* she greeted them.

As Danielle lifted her head, Rodmilla smiled down at her, a cool, perfunctory smile. "Hello, Danielle." Her voice was smooth. "At last we meet. Your father speaks of nothing else." She paused, her eyes flickering from the comb that dangled haphazardly from Danielle's hair to the mud that spattered her skirt. "Although, for a moment there, I thought I was meeting a little boy."

Auguste stepped forward. "Yes, well, a father's influence can be a blessing and a curse. She has things to learn only a gentlewoman can teach her."

Danielle bit her lip as her father reached forward and touched Rodmilla's cheek. Surely if her father liked this woman, she would too. Wouldn't she?

Rodmilla examined Danielle, seemingly memorizing every unsatisfactory detail. "I will do what I can with her," she said abruptly. She turned to her daughters. "Ladies, say hello to your new stepsister."

Danielle watched as the two girls curtsied in unison. As they raised their chins, Danielle gave them a tentative but heartfelt smile. *Christmas day!* she thought, trying to find the exuberance that had filled her only minutes before.

But as the chilly eyes of Marguerite and Jacqueline stared back at her, Danielle could find only one feeling.

Fear.

Danielle's fingers moved slowly across the book's engraved gold lettering. "'Utopia,'" she read, looking to her father for explanation. The book had been an unexpected gift, given to her in the privacy of her bedroom. Her father always made sure to stop in and kiss her goodnight.

"It means paradise," he told her, patting its cover. "A bit thick for an eight-year-old, but I thought we could add it to our library."

"Will you read some?" Danielle asked, lying back and propping herself up on her elbows. A fire crackled in the fireplace, casting a warm glow around the room.

Her father shook his head. "My dear, it has been a very long day."

Danielle sighed as she remembered she was no longer the only woman in her father's life. "And you are a husband now."

Auguste de Barbarac brushed a tendril of hair from his daughter's face. "A husband, true, but a father first and forever. We have been two peas in a pod, you and I. For a long time, I suppose, this will take some getting used to."

Danielle's heart warmed at her father's words. "Did you see the way they ate their supper?" she asked. Her stepsisters' portions had been so small, their bites so dainty, their movements so carefully orchestrated. Danielle had felt a regular rustic as she'd crunched through her vegetables and cut and chewed her chicken. "It was perfect. Like a dance."

Auguste peered intently into Danielle's face. "Do you like them?"

"Very much," she said. *Or at least, I hope I will,* she thought worriedly.

"Good. Because I must go to Avignon in a fortnight."

She sat bolt upright. "But you just got back!"

"I know."

Her eyes narrowed. "How long will you be away?"

"Three weeks."

Danielle folded her arms across her chest. "One."

Her father chuckled. "Two."

"One," she insisted stubbornly. As if on cue, they each formed a fist with their right hand, put the fist behind their back, and counted to three. "Rock, paper, scissors!" They drew.

"Paper covers rock!" Danielle crowed, putting her tiny hand over her father's fist and squeezing.

A grin spread across his face. "All right, one week." He leaned forward and kissed her on the forehead. "Now go to bed." After quickly checking the fire, he was gone, closing the bedroom door softly behind him.

With a happy smile, Danielle settled under her soft down comforter. "Utopia," she whispered as she drifted off to sleep. "Utopia."

A slight film of dust covered the old cedar chest that sat against the wall in Rodmilla's new bedchamber. Rodmilla studied it in silence, then raised the heavy lid. Dresses of Parisian silk, eggshell-thin bone china, and smooth bolts of Belgian linen greeted her.

"My, my." She fingered a delicate pink teacup. As she moved forward to get a better look at the chest's contents, a shaft of moonlight fell on a small pair of silver satin slippers covered with a thousand tiny crystal beads. Whoever had worn them must have had the feet of fairies, Rodmilla mused. They were so dainty and delicate. Brushing them aside, she lifted out a beautiful beaded evening gown. She held it up against herself and let out a tiny gasp of delight. The slippers would never fit her, but the dress, the dress was exquisite. The baroness smiled. This gown would catch every eye in the kingdom, with its puckered folds fitting tightly across the breast, its beads catching the light, its—

A movement in the doorway startled her.

"Auguste!"

His eyes lingered on the dress as if calling back a distant memory. "Nicole wore it at our wedding."

"Ah, then this would be Danielle's dowry." Rodmilla folded the dress in two, returned it to its place in the chest, and closed the lid. "It must be very painful to lose one love just as another enters the world," she said, moving toward her husband. "Such tragedy mixed with such joy."

Danielle's mother had died during childbirth. She must have been a beautiful but ultimately a weak woman, Rodmilla had concluded.

Auguste took his new wife's hand. "And now love has found me again."

"But Auguste, honestly. This house, the memories . . ." She gestured at the room around them. "The distance from town. When my husband died, God rest his soul, I packed up immediately."

"Yes, but darling, he was convicted of treason," Auguste reminded her. "You would have been beheaded right along with him."

Rodmilla sniffed. "Well, that was a long time ago, and now I have you. All to myself. Finally." She moved into his arms, kissing his cheek and nuzzling his neck. Auguste was so strong, so handsome, but so . . . unambitious. She smiled to herself. She could change that.

"Careful, *madame*," Auguste whispered, nuzzling her in return. "You know not what you do."

Rodmilla kissed his nose. "I think at my age I know exactly what I am doing." Then his cheek. "Oh, darling, I cannot wait until we're introduced at court." Next his earlobe. "I understand the king has a son about Marguerite's age." Then his lips. "Wouldn't that be something?" she purred.

Auguste laughed. "Good God, woman, you just got here."

Rodmilla wrapped her hands around his neck. "I'm doing this for us, dear. You know the old saying, 'A good wife sets sail according to the keel of her husband's estate'? Well, we need a bigger boat."

Auguste gave her an admiring look. "You've already won over Danielle. She thinks you're positively regal."

Rodmilla raised her perfectly plucked eyebrows. "*Au contraire,* I think she is the one wearing the crown in this house." It hadn't escaped her eye that the servants seemed to cater to the scrappy little urchin.

"Can you blame me?" Auguste asked, looking at her with puppy-dog eyes.

Rodmilla could, but she wouldn't. Not just yet. She'd have to wait until she was firmly established in Auguste's house before whipping things into shape. "Honestly, Auguste," she said instead, tickling him playfully in the ribs. "She's a little boy."

Auguste fell onto the bed, drawing his new wife to him. "You should see her with a sword."

Danielle fought back the lump that had formed in her throat and tried to look brave. Her father had left on dozens of trips, but it still didn't make saying goodbye any easier. She sneaked a peek at Jacqueline and Marguerite. They didn't look sad at all. *That's because they don't know how much fun Papa is,* Danielle told herself. *They'll sure be in for a surprise when he comes back and we all begin doing things together!*

Auguste fastened his heavy cloak around his neck and pulled on his leather riding gloves. His gaze swept over the somber line of servants, then across his family. "I have never seen so many gloomy faces," he said, the cheerfulness of his tone telling them everything would be all right. "I shall be back in a week." He bent to kiss Rodmilla.

"Then go," Rodmilla said, clasping him tightly and then abruptly releasing him. "The sooner you leave, the sooner we can celebrate your return."

Danielle scuffed her new shoe in the dirt. Her father kissed Marguerite and Jacqueline on the cheek and then stooped down to her. "Perhaps by then you three will have gotten to know each other better," he said, hugging her. Danielle hugged him back, feeling suddenly small and alone.

"I am counting on you to teach them the ropes around here," he instructed his daughter. He turned to Rodmilla. "The baroness isn't used to getting her hands dirty," he teased.

Danielle looked at her stepmother's lily-white fingers. She could believe that.

Danielle stood there, watching, as her father mounted his horse and trotted down the dirt driveway that led to the main road. It was going to be hard having these three strangers in her house, but she would do as her father asked. He would be proud of her.

Rodmilla clapped her hands. "Come along, ladies. Back to your lessons." Her skirt swished as she took her daughters by the hand.

"Wait," Danielle piped up. "He always waves when he gets to the gate. It's a tradition."

The baroness paused for a moment, then dismissed the idea, heading into the house. So Danielle stood steadfastly without her new stepmother and stepsisters and, along with the staff, watched her father depart. Her father would expect her to be there.

Danielle waited for his goodbye wave. He had

almost reached the gate—that was when he normally turned. That day, he did not.

That day, he slumped over and tumbled from his horse.

"Papa!" Danielle shrieked. Her tiny face contorted with fear. She ran down the path toward him, Maurice by her side. This couldn't be happening. Papa was so strong, so healthy . . . he wouldn't be taken ill just like that, would he?

Auguste de Barbarac was lying facedown in the dust, his horse nervously pawing the ground beside him. Maurice turned him over, and Danielle began to sob. Her father's face was pale, and his breath was ragged. Danielle fell to the ground beside him, her body racked with sobs. *Please, Papa,* she begged, grabbing his arm. *Please don't die. I love you too much. Please . . .*

Rodmilla came running up beside them and pushed Maurice and Danielle aside. "Auguste, please, you cannot leave me here!" she cried, clutching his cloak.

Auguste stared up helplessly into his new wife's face . . . and then reached out for Danielle. But it was too late. His hands grasped the air in vain and then fell limply to his side. His mouth went slack.

Frightened, Danielle looked up at Rodmilla for some comfort, tears streaking her face.

Angry that her husband's dying gesture had been for his daughter and not her, Rodmilla stamped back up the drive. She was off to take a thorough look at the house—*her* house now. Her posture was ramrod straight, her stony gaze focused straight ahead.

Filled with a despair she had never known, Danielle buried her head in her father's chest, soaking his lifeless body with tears. In a matter of minutes the most important person in the world had been cruelly snatched away from her.

Her precious father was dead.

And, she, Danielle de Barbarac, was an orphan.

Chapter One
1512

The frosty night air sent a shock through Henry's system as he hoisted his bedchamber window, but he was not about to turn back. Pulling his hood up over his head, he climbed out and began to make his way down the cold stone wall of Hautefort. This wasn't the first time he had attempted an escape, but it would be the last. He had to succeed.

His heart depended on it.

Forbidding himself to look down, he moved slowly but surely, gripping each crevice with his fingertips. As he reached the second floor, his eyes were drawn to the salamander emblem and initials inscribed above the west chamber's window: F & M. Francis and Marie, his parents.

Or, as they were known to the rest of the world, King Francis and Queen Marie of France.

Taking a deep breath, Henry slipped past the window, inside which his father's angry voice rang out. "I signed a marriage treaty with the King of Spain, and by God, that boy will obey my command or there will be hell to pay!" A door slammed, and soon the sound of clattering shoes crossing the courtyard echoed up to Henry.

"He does not love her, milord," his mother's voice pleaded.

"It's not about love." His father was imperious.

Henry winced.

"Perhaps it should be," his mother replied innocently.

For a moment Henry hesitated. He loved his parents deeply . . . but not deeply enough to marry someone he had no feelings for. If only his father would come around, would see how insane it would be for Henry to marry—

"If he is to be king he needs to accept his responsibilities!" his father's voice boomed.

Henry quickly moved on down the wall. It was no use. His father would never change.

"A sapling cannot grow in the shadow of a mighty oak, Francis. He needs sunlight," his mother argued.

19

"He needs a good whipping!" his father thundered.

Henry jumped the remaining few feet to the ground, startling an unassuming guardsman on night watch, at the ready with a horse. Without a word, the young prince swung himself up on the horse and galloped off into the darkness.

"Cock-a-doodle-doo! Cock-a-doodle-doo!"

At the sound of the rooster's crowing, the young woman who lay asleep in front of the fireplace stirred. The fire had gone out, and now all that was left was the soot that stained her clothes and face and the faint smell of embers that drifted through the house.

Yawning, she sat up and stretched, running a tired hand through her long brown hair and rubbing her eyes. Morning had come much too soon. Carefully she took the book that had lain open on her chest and closed it. Years of nightly reading had taken their toll on the pages, and the leather cover, once smooth and rich, was pockmarked. Long golden threads dangled from the binding.

With a sigh, the young woman wiped the book with her apron and placed it on the mantel. *Utopia* was its title.

Another day had dawned.

Time for Danielle to get to work.

* * *

Is this the sixth bucket or the seventh? Danielle wondered as she poured a pailful of water onto the withering crops that lay to the side of the Manoir de Barbarac. Not that it mattered. For years Danielle had been trying to keep the once lush gardens and orchards alive, but the prospects dimmed with each passing winter. How could one girl keep an entire estate in bloom?

Keeping her spirits alive was hard enough.

After she had finished chopping enough firewood for the day, Danielle made her way to the orchard. Thankfully, her father's apple trees were still generous with their bounty, and she could always count on finding enough apples for one of the cooks to bake into a tart or chop for applesauce.

Using her apron as a makeshift basket, Danielle began to gather the fruit. When she'd collected enough, she headed back toward the manor, enjoying her solitude on this early morning. The sun was fully risen, and the light spilled over the manor's roof, making her smile.

A loud whinny from the stables startled her. She blinked in bewilderment as her father's old black stallion came racing from the stables, leaped over a brambly hedge, and galloped straight for her. A hooded, cloaked figure sat hunched on the horse's back, urging it forward.

Danielle was enraged. Instinctively she grabbed an apple and hurled it at the oncoming rider. To her satisfaction, she hit him squarely between his thick eyebrows. The unanticipated blow knocked him backward off the horse.

As the dazed rider stumbled to his feet, Danielle fired off more apples. "Thief!" she cried. "This will teach you to steal my father's horse."

"Please, my own has thrown his shoe and I have no choice!" the man cried.

"And our choice is what?" Danielle shouted, her brown eyes flashing. "To let you do this?" How dared this impudent man think he could burst into what had been her father's house and steal his most prized horse? The thought infuriated her, and she began to throw the rest of her apples at him.

The hooded figure ran for cover behind the horse, which refused to stay put, whinnying and scratching in the dirt.

"Wait!" the man yelled, trying to shield himself from an apple. "Ow!"

"Get out!" Danielle shrieked.

"I was merely borrowing the horse!" he protested.

Ignoring his pleas, Danielle flung another apple. "Shoo! Or I'll wake the whole house!"

The stallion reared up, knocking the man

to the ground. Danielle hurried over, an apple clasped in her hand, ready to pelt him again if necessary.

His hood had fallen back, and Danielle got a good look at his face.

Despite her anger, she couldn't help noticing that the young man who stared into her eyes was gorgeous. Chiseled cheekbones, soft red lips, dark eyes with equally dark lashes, and soft, silky black hair that just grazed his shoulders.

A lump of panic began to form in her stomach. Danielle recognized this face . . . this face had smiled broadly from parades, these hands had waved at crowds, this handsome body had sat upon the most regal of horses. . . .

This was no thief. This was Prince Henry, son of the King of France!

Danielle threw herself to the ground in front of him. "Forgive me, Your Highness, I did not see you!" she cried. Tears welled up in her eyes. How could she have done such a stupid thing— throwing apples at the prince!

"Your aim would suggest otherwise," the prince said dryly.

"And for that I know I must die!" Her heart was beating so fast she thought it would burst through her chest.

Prince Henry looked around them, then rose

to his knees. "Then speak of this to no one, and I shall be lenient."

Did he really mean it? Danielle's mouth hung agape as the prince quickly scanned the area, then remounted the horse.

"We have others, Highness. Younger horses, if that is your wish," Danielle told him, her eyes on the ground.

He opened a leather pouch and poured a heap of gold coins on the dirt. Her eyes opened wide at the fortune that lay scattered in the dust.

"I wish for nothing more than to be free of my gilded cage," he said softly.

His words were odd, and for a second she was tempted to ask him what he meant. But the prince had already galloped off.

Was she dreaming? Had this truly occurred? Danielle quickly gathered the coins, squeezing one between her dirty fingers. *Real gold coins . . . and they're mine!* she thought dizzily. A smile lit up her face. She knew just what to do with them.

Picking up a few of the apples, she raced to the manor and dashed inside the kitchen door. Paulette and Louise were busily slicing bread and spooning jam into tiny crocks. Their eyes shot question marks at Danielle, but before she could explain, a call came from the dining room.

"Why is there no salt on this table?" Rod-

24

milla's loud voice demanded. Danielle's step-mother sounded irate, even for her.

"Coming!" Danielle called, spilling the apples onto the worn wooden work table. She grabbed a block of salt from the hutch and began scraping it into a salt bowl.

"She is in one of her moods," Paulette said under her breath.

Louise rolled her eyes. "Did the sun rise in the east?" They were so used to Rodmilla's bad attitude that a kind word or look would have sent them into shock.

"Yes, Louise, it did," Danielle replied brightly. "And it is going to be a beautiful day." She pulled a handful of coins out of her apron pocket.

Paulette's eyes widened. "Look at all those feathers!" She clutched Danielle's arm. "Child, where did you get these?"

"From an angel of mercy." Danielle looked straight at Louise. "And I know just what to do with them."

"Maurice!" Louise covered her mouth and promptly burst into tears.

"If the baroness can sell your husband to pay her taxes, then this can certainly bring him home." Danielle's face shone with conviction. "The court will have to let him go."

"But the king sold him to Cartier," Louise

murmured through her tears. "Maurice is bound for the Americas."

"Not yet, he isn't." Danielle stood tall. "This is *our* home, and I will not see it fall apart."

Rodmilla's shrill voice rose from the dining room. "We are waiting," she called.

Paulette leaned close. "Take heed, mistress," she warned Danielle, "or those coins are as good as hers."

Danielle nodded. Her friend was right. If Rodmilla learned of the fortune she'd acquired, it would be stripped from her within seconds. Hurriedly she stuffed the money back into her apron pocket, picked up the salt, and entered the dining room.

"Morning, *madame*. Marguerite. Jacqueline. I trust you slept well."

Rodmilla picked up a piece of bread. "What kept you?"

Danielle paused. "I . . . um . . . fell off the ladder in the orchard, but I am better now." She cautiously placed the salt next to Marguerite, biting her lip as a few flakes of ash fell onto the snow-white tablecloth.

"Someone's been reading in the fireplace again," Marguerite sneered. "Look at you, ash and soot everywhere."

Rodmilla took a sip of coffee. "Some people read because they cannot think for themselves."

"Why don't you sleep with the pigs, Cindersoot, if you insist on smelling like one?" Marguerite taunted, spooning salt onto her plate.

Danielle bit back a reply. Her stepsister wasn't worth the trouble.

Rodmilla sent her daughter an admonishing look. "That was harsh, Marguerite. Danielle, come here, child."

Danielle walked slowly toward her stepmother, wondering what would be found wrong with her that day.

"Your appearance does reflect a certain . . . crudeness, my dear," Rodmilla said, taking in the soot, dirt, and tangled hair. "What can I do to make you try?"

Perhaps give me a bed to sleep in, a basin to wash my face in, and a morning when I can sleep past six, Danielle thought with a twinge of bitterness. "I do try, Stepmother," she replied, her voice shaking. Even though her stepmother had proved to be no friend, Danielle couldn't give up hope that one day she would show some kindness, some small recognition that Danielle was a person, that she had feelings just like anyone else. "I—I do wish to please you. Sometimes I sit on my own and try to think of what else I could do, how I should act—"

Rodmilla held up a hand. "Calm yourself, child. Relax."

Danielle mustered her courage. "Perhaps if we brought back Maurice, I would not offend you so." Maurice had always helped her, had always offered advice when she needed it and none when she didn't. If only—

"It is your manner that offends, Danielle," Rodmilla said sharply, clanging her coffee cup on its saucer. "In these hard times, I have sheltered you, clothed you, cared for you. All I ask in return is that you help me here without complaint. Is it such an extraordinary request?"

Danielle flushed. "No, milady."

"Then I will hear no more talk of servants coming back. Is that understood?"

"Yes, milady." With a short curtsy, Danielle excused herself. As she pushed open the door into the kitchen, her stepmother's parting words rang in her ears.

"After all I have done," she heard Rodmilla complain. "After all that I do. It is never enough for the likes of her."

Chapter Two

The stallion was spirited for his age, and Henry had given him full rein, allowing him to gallop down one forest trail after another. Henry understood what having that kind of freedom meant, being able to choose one's own road. He reached forward and gave the horse's sweaty neck a gentle rub. As soon as he came to a stream, he'd allow the thirsty animal to have a drink.

As he slowed the tiring stallion with a tightening of the reins, Henry's thoughts drifted back to the scene earlier that morning. What good aim that servant girl had, flinging apples at him as if he were the target of a firing squad. And how bravely she had defended her master's property. It must be something to feel that much emotion over a possession. Henry might have been a prince, but he felt a strange lack of attachment to what he had. His bedchamber at Hautefort was filled with riches . . . heavy, ornate tapestries; woodcarvings from Flanders and Spain; a writing desk inlaid with tortoiseshell and pearls . . . but Henry would give it all away to be free. Then he grinned to himself as he reached into his pocket and felt the empty leather pouch. *Would* give it away? He *had* given it away. He was free.

Where would he go? The south of France was warm, but too close . . . he could easily be found. Considering his marriage prospects, Spain was out of the question. Italy . . . a couple of months basking in the Tuscan sun, drinking wine and feasting on sun-ripened tomatoes and delicious pastas, visiting the picturesque countryside . . . a stay there could be just what he needed. Not that it would take the place of love . . . but then, he'd never been in love in the first place.

In the distance, a glimmer of color between the trees caught his eye. A scruffy band of Gypsies had surrounded what appeared to be an old man. Henry watched, disturbed, as they rifled the old man's things, tossing them from one Gypsy to the next. True, Henry had been a thief of sorts that morning, but he would never do anything to harm an elder. That was going too far.

Henry moved closer. Could he defend himself against the group? One man against twelve? He was still trying to decide when, to his surprise, one of the Gypsies looked his way, then quickly whistled to his men. They scattered in all directions.

Henry sat taller in his saddle and straightened his cloak. Who needed a sword and a suit of armor? One look at him and the Gypsies had fled as if the entire royal guard had been about to swoop down.

Hooves thundered behind him, and Henry turned.

The royal guard *was* about to swoop down. But not on the pack of Gypsies.

On him.

Henry gave the stallion a sharp kick. "Go!" he cried, smacking the reins against the fatigued horse's neck.

Before he could escape, the old man hurried over, his robes dragging in the dust. Coarse white hair spilled over his shoulders, and his beard was scraggly.

"Please, for the love of God, the painting!" His eyes were wild. "That man, there, he's getting away!" He pointed to the Gypsy leader, who had taken off on foot through the trees, a brass tube clutched in his grimy hands.

"The guard will assist you!" Henry exclaimed, looking back over his shoulder. They had almost reached him. "I cannot!"

To his dismay, the old man grabbed his leg. "Please, sir, it is my life."

What could be so important about a painting? Henry was ready to shake the crazed fool off and gallop away. Each second he wasted brought him closer to certain capture. But something in the old man's eyes reached him. It was the same look the apple-throwing maiden had had . . . a look of pride, desperation, and . . . humanity.

Cursing his weakness, Henry gave the old man a curt nod and took off into the woods after the Gypsy thief.

The bandit had a good lead, and Henry had his work cut out for him. He guided the stallion uphill through the tangle of trees and branches, the Gypsy's brightly colored tunic his bull's-eye. Briars stuck to his clothing, and as a wayward branch smacked him in the face, Henry swore. Gallantry was the stuff of silly storybooks. Maybe he should just give up, go back, and tell the old man he'd lost the Gypsy. Not that that would be the most honorable thing to do, but at least he'd be spared any further injury.

He closed his eyes and breathed deeply as the

horse came to a stop on a small crest. Thankfully, Henry opened his eyes in time to see the thief, now on horseback himself, take a mighty swing at him with a huge stick.

Dodging the blow, Henry managed to control his horse as the Gypsy galloped off into the forest.

"Yaaaa!" Henry shouted, spurring the stallion to follow.

The chase was on.

Trees, boulders, hedges . . . all was a blur as Henry and the Gypsy careened wildly through the trees. The brass tube dangled from the Gypsy's arms. Henry had never been so bent on getting something back in his life. He leaned so low on the horse that he was practically hugging it, hoping that the sure-footed stallion would have the strength to continue.

Within seconds they had broken free of the trees, and Henry realized that the forest was on the side of a mountain.

Then he realized that the two horses were racing toward a narrow pathway that ran around the side of the mountain.

With the Gypsy just a fraction of a second ahead of him, Henry reached forward and curled his fingers around the elusive brass tube.

And then it was too late.

With loud cries, the two men sailed off their horses, plummeting a short distance to the mucky pond that lay adjacent to their path.

Cold water sent shivers through Henry's body as he broke the surface. Shaking the water from his face and victoriously clutching the brass tube, he began to swim to shore with strong, clean strokes.

"Aggh!" Henry gagged as a wet, tunic-clad arm reached around him from behind, attempting to put him in a headlock. He struggled to stand up in the shallow water, then did the only thing he could think of.

He twisted around and clubbed the man unconscious with the brass tube.

One marvelous thing about living in France was that bakeries were never in short supply. Jacqueline bit into her second—or was it her third?—chocolate éclair and tried to remember which it was. She'd been standing on the street corner at the alley's end for so long she'd lost count. She didn't particularly like being a lookout while her mother and Marguerite got to pick through the shady gold vendor's wares out of sight. "I don't want anyone we know to see us here, Jacqueline," her mother had instructed her.

"Dealing with an alley merchant, well, that's not the kind of thing we should be known for."

Jacqueline licked a thin residue of chocolate from her fingertips. So they couldn't afford fancy jewels from the fine shops in town. Was that a crime? She peered into her bag. *Let's see, should it be the fig tart or the cream puff?* She closed her eyes and reached into the bag. *The cream puff!* Raising the delicious treat to her mouth, she spotted two well-dressed ladies coming down the street . . . Celeste and Isabelle, the most important noblewomen in town! Her mother would be furious if Jacqueline didn't warn her and Marguerite that they were about to be spotted with the cheap alley merchant.

Shoving her pastry back into its bag, Jacqueline brought her fingers to her mouth to let out a warning whistle . . . but all she got was a dribble of crumbs and a small puff of powdered sugar. Frantic, she tried to think of something else to do, but nothing came to her, and soon the two women were gliding past.

Jacqueline leaned nonchalantly against a nearby building, then peered down the darkened alley to find her mother and sister. The noblewomen's eyes widened at the shifty shopping spree taking place.

"Honestly, Rodmilla, a young lady's reputation

does not belong in an alleyway," Celeste said reprovingly from the safety of the street, nodding toward Marguerite.

Marguerite clutched a medium-sized gold brooch and looked nervously at her mother. The gold vendor scurried out of sight.

Rodmilla was contrite. "All right, I'll confess, I was bargain shopping for my chambermaids."

"Gifts for the help," Isabelle murmured, her tone doubtful. "What a novel idea." She called to Rodmilla, "I suppose you've already heard. The prince has run away."

"He wants to marry for love!" Celeste chuckled, amazed. "Can you imagine? Why, the very idea is—"

"Crude and utterly selfish," Rodmilla finished.

Jacqueline sighed. The whole thing sounded utterly romantic to her.

"I wonder if anyone has caught his eye?" Isabelle put in.

A change came over Rodmilla's face as the gold vendor returned with an enormous brooch. "Mmmm," she replied slowly, her eyes roving from Jacqueline to Marguerite. "I wonder."

"Have you lost your marbles?" Gustave shook his head. "Do you know what the punishment is for servants who dress above their station? Five days in the stocks!"

Danielle leaned out from behind the screen inside her friend's cramped painting studio and stuck out her lip. "You'd do the same for me. Admit it."

"*Me?*" Gustave was incredulous. "Pretend to be a courtier? Prancing around like a nobleman? Why, I've never even been to court." He wagged his finger at her. "And neither have you."

"Then I won't be recognized. Now, hand me that gown so I can be on my way."

Luck was on her side that day. Gustave had been commissioned to paint the portrait of an old, very rich noblewoman. After her sitting, the woman had allowed Gustave to keep one of her gowns, as well as some of her jewels, so that he could consult them at his leisure while he completed the portrait. Danielle had sneaked over to the studio to borrow the gown and jewels, complete her mission, and return them, with no one except Gustave the wiser.

She hoped she'd be as lucky on her mission. Dressed like a royal courtier, and carrying a purseful of gold coins, she was sure she could persuade the king to let Maurice go. If not—well, she didn't want to think about it. As she'd left that morning, Louise's face had been so full of hope, of trust, that Danielle knew she couldn't return home if she failed.

"The gown?" she asked Gustave impatiently.

With a disapproving scowl, Gustave handed over the silken bundle. "They'll never believe you. You're not snotty enough."

"I will just have to be convincing. I am his only hope," Danielle replied, stepping into the heavy brocaded skirt.

"And the baroness?" Gustave wrinkled his nose. "What did you tell her?"

"That I'm picking wildflowers." Danielle peeked around the screen as she adjusted the gown's bodice. "Can you still see her?" Who would have guessed her stepmother and stepsisters would be lurking about in an alley in Gustave's neighborhood?

Gustave looked out the window. "They're buying a brooch."

Danielle let out a disgusted sigh as she tightened the dress's laces. "Unbelievable. She ignores the manor, blames me and the staff for her debt, and still pretends to have money to burn." She gave the skirt a tug. "Now, don't you dare laugh. I'm coming out."

Danielle stepped out from behind the screen.

Suddenly she felt silly. Gustave was right. This was a terrible idea. Who would ever believe that she, Cindersoot, was a courtier, a noble? "The shoes are too big," she mumbled, fussing with the buckles. Slowly she raised her eyes, waiting for the expected jokes.

They never came.

"Nobody will be looking at your feet," Gustave whispered, obviously stunned.

Danielle could feel her cheeks flush. "Yards of fabric, and I still feel naked," she said, gesturing to her bared shoulders and décolletage.

"If you are going to be a noblewoman, you must play the part." Gustave lifted Danielle's chin. "You look down for no one. Keep your eyes and chin up at all times."

"I am just a servant in a nice dress," Danielle said, embarrassed.

Gustave started to speak, then clamped his mouth shut. "Come," he said simply. "We have to fix your hair."

"Henry, you promised," Captain Laurent said sorrowfully.

Henry hung his head. "I know. I lied." Yes, he'd been able to return the brass tube to its rightful owner . . . but the act had cost him his freedom.

The entire royal guard surrounded him, with his father's captain doing the real dirty work: giving him a major tongue-lashing.

"I thought I'd see the world before I gave up my life to God and country," Henry added, his dreams crashing at his soaking wet feet.

"Then why did you stop?" the old man asked. By now he had unscrewed the end of the tube and pulled out the rolled canvas.

Henry shrugged. "I suppose it's because I lack conviction. You seem to have it in spades. You claimed it was a matter of life and death."

The old man smiled. "A woman always is, sire." With a flourish, he unfurled the painting.

Henry stared at the portrait of a woman with long black hair, a full face, and a strange, almost mysterious smile. "She laughs at me, sir, as if she knows something I do not."

"The lady had many secrets," the old man replied. "I merely painted one of them."

Captain Laurent cleared his throat. "Signore da Vinci has been invited to the palace as artist-in-residence."

Henry's jaw dropped. Could it really be . . . "Leonardo da Vinci?"

The old man smiled at the prince. "Michelangelo was busy with a ceiling in Rome. I am but a second choice."

Henry's spirits soared. "Why, here I am on my way to Genoa and I find my salvation on the highway!" he burst out, grabbing the famous artist by the shoulders. "Sir, you are the very founder of forward thinking, and my father is the king of backward thinking! Perhaps you can talk him into the sixteenth century!"

Leonardo looked confused. "Captain Laurent, do translate."

"Prince Henry suffers from an arranged marriage, *signore*," the captain explained. "Among other things."

The artist nodded wisely. "Ah."

Think clearly, think logically, Rodmilla commanded herself. She took a deep breath and tried to forget that the royal guard, along with one of the world's most noted artists, was standing outside the manor's main gate . . . and that the prince himself, accompanied by one of his staff, was walking down the lane.

It was impossible.

She smoothed back her glossy black hair and straightened her dress. Marguerite stood gaping at the prince through the drawing room window. Rodmilla cupped Marguerite's face. *This* was the daughter with potential . . . with Marguerite's face and figure, she could easily win the heart of any man. The prince would surely succumb to her charms if mother and daughter played their cards right.

"Change quickly, girl," Rodmilla said, her eyes bright, "and do so with utmost care, for you are about to meet your future husband."

Marguerite let out a half gasp, half giggle.

"Remember, courtesy is currency," Rodmilla added, swatting her on the behind and gesturing toward Marguerite's bedchamber. "Now go!"

Then Rodmilla's glance fell on Jacqueline, who stood hovering in the background. "You! Help her!"

The baroness wondered why she, of all people, had ended up not only with a vile stepdaughter like Danielle, but also with a flesh-and-blood daughter like Jacqueline, who was so . . . so . . . so *gauche*.

But this was no time to dwell on misfortune.

Because Rodmilla had a feeling her ship had finally sailed into port.

"Your Highness, what a lovely surprise," Rodmilla said, rising from her curtsy and bestowing her most charming smile on the prince, who for some reason seemed to be slightly wet. Not that it mattered. "I wasn't expecting such handsome company." She gestured to the room around her, which had just undergone the fastest sweeping, polishing, and tidying up it had ever had. "To what do we owe this honor?"

Prince Henry smiled. "I am returning your horse, Baroness."

"Oh . . ." Rodmilla was puzzled. "Was it missing?"

"Yes, I borrowed it this morning," he replied. "I'm afraid I might have scared the wits out of one of your servants—a young lady with quite a good arm, actually."

Cold hatred washed over Rodmilla. That scheming stepdaughter of hers . . . "She is mute, Your Highness," she explained, trying to achieve just the right note of pity and dismissiveness.

"Really?" The prince raised his eyebrows. "She spoke quite forcefully."

Rodmilla held up her hands. "It comes and goes." She looked at him coyly. "But as always, His Highness is welcome to anything he wishes. Anything at all."

As if on cue, Marguerite burst into the drawing room, eyes wild and hair disheveled, a panic-stricken Jacqueline on her heels. Rodmilla forced away the tight, strained smile that naturally appeared on her lips, and instead gave her daughter

43

the most approving of looks. *Better to keep her re-laxed . . . much easier to make a good impression on the prince that way. And at least she had the good sense to wear her most revealing gown.*

"Oh, hello, ladies," Rodmilla said gracefully, as if the prince dropped by every day. "Look who's here."

"Your Highness," the sisters said in unison, dropping to the floor in a synchronized curtsy.

Rodmilla turned to the prince. "May I present Marguerite Françoise Louise of the House of Ghent?"

Marguerite beamed. Jacqueline gave a tiny, self-conscious cough.

"Oh, and Jacqueline," Rodmilla added, barely noticing the smile that Captain Laurent gave her younger daughter. Rodmilla was too busy planning her next move.

"You may present them indeed," Prince Henry said. "Ladies, forgive me, but you seem to have blossomed overnight."

Rodmilla stepped a fraction of an inch closer to the prince. "We are so looking forward to celebrating your engagement to your own Spanish rose."

"Yes, well, there have been several . . . new de-velopments," he said vaguely. To Rodmilla's intense pleasure, the young prince seemed to be taken with Marguerite's new brooch, affixed firmly to the bodice of her dress . . . right above her ample bosom. "I must say, Marguerite, that brooch is stunning," he commented.

"This old thing?" Marguerite cooed. "You are too kind."

Rodmilla resisted the urge to wink at her daughter. "These developments, I trust, are for the best?" she asked the prince, batting her eyes.

Prince Henry paused. "Let us hope so. Good day."

"W-Would you like to come in and get out of those wet clothes?" Jacqueline blurted out.

Rodmilla whipped her head around and saw a blushing, stammering Jacqueline. Shooting her a furious glare, she turned to apologize to the prince for her daughter's rude candor. But he looked bemused, not angry.

"That's a lovely offer, Jacqueline," he said kindly. "But I fear I would never want to leave." With a small bow, the prince walked out of the manor, Captain Laurent a pace behind.

Rodmilla drew back the curtain and watched as the two men, Signore da Vinci, and the royal guard galloped off.

On the whole, the unexpected visit had gone

quite well . . . and she was one step closer to getting her leather-booted toe into the castle. Then Rodmilla's eyes narrowed. How dared Danielle keep secret the fact that the prince had borrowed one of their horses?

The little fool would pay.

Chapter Three

"**I**'m really here," Danielle whispered. "I'm doing this." She had seen Hautefort hundreds of times, but that day the castle looked even more imposing than it had before. *Probably because this is the first time I've ever actually had a prayer of getting inside,* she thought nervously. Rumor had it that the castle had more than four hundred rooms and three hundred fireplaces, not to mention the thousands of acres of royal land that surrounded it. Hurrying toward the main gate, she stopped, took a deep breath, and began to walk like a lady. *Courtiers don't run up to the palace gates,* she told herself. They floated.

Or tried to.

A horde of peasants had surrounded the

castle's outer gates, and for a moment Danielle's heart plummeted. She hadn't expected such crowds. But then a guardsman spotted her and motioned to her to step forward. Danielle touched her hair, which Gustave had pulled back with a jeweled clasp. She smoothed the gown of cream, gold, and silver brocaded satin and velvet and adjusted the gold cord circling her waist. Gustave's magic had worked! She was in!

She crossed the drawbridge that led to the castle's front gates, passing weapon-toting guardsmen. Her hands, slick with hand cream Gustave had insisted she apply, began to sweat. The castle looked very different from inside the high iron outer gates. Blue-capped turrets seemed to scrape the sky, and a huge entranceway overlooked the courtyard. Immense manicured gardens lay on either side, one with a fountain. Window after window gleamed in the light, the thick glass a sharp contrast with the snow-white marble of the castle walls.

The graceful beauty of the castle stunned her.

So too did the sight of her old friend Maurice being herded like a cow onto a prison wagon.

Danielle looked to the heavens. "God give me strength," she muttered. Then, without hesitation, she hurried to intercept the wagon as it came around the corner toward the main gate.

She held up her hand, and the wagon was forced to slow. "This gentleman is my servant, and I am here to pay the debt against him," she declared, pointing at the confused Maurice.

"Too late," the wagon master barked, his fleshy cheeks swaying as he shook his head. "Bought and paid for."

The sight of her friend behind the prison wagon's bars was almost too much to bear. How could anyone treat such a kind, good man this way? To her consternation, Danielle watched a flash of recognition appear on the head steward's face. His hands gripped the bars of his cage so tightly that they turned white. Danielle hoped he would realize what she was trying to do and stay quiet.

"I can pay you twenty gold francs," she informed the wagon master in the haughtiest voice she could muster.

To her dismay, he threw his head back and laughed. "*Madame,* you can have *me* for twenty gold francs." Craning his thick neck, he yelled to the driver, "Drive on!"

He doesn't believe I have that kind of money, Danielle thought frantically. In desperation, she grabbed the horse's bridle. "I demand you release him at once, or . . . or . . . I shall, uh, take this matter to the king!"

"The king's the one who sold him—now he's the property of Cartier." The wagon master's face had flushed deep crimson.

"He is not property at all, you ill-mannered tub of guts!" Danielle exclaimed.

A murmur went up from the crowd of courtiers that had begun to form around them. "Do you honestly think it right to chain people like chattel?" Danielle drew a breath. "I demand you release him at once!"

"Get out of my way!" the wagon master bellowed.

"You dare raise your voice to a lady, sir?" said a deep baritone from somewhere in the crowd.

Danielle turned and saw the masses part and then bow as Prince Henry strode toward them, accompanied by a tall, immaculately dressed guardsman. Quickly she lowered her head. If the prince recognized her as the girl who had thrown apples at him, she could forget about buying Maurice's freedom . . . she'd likely be locked up herself!

"Forgive me, Your Highness," the wagon master whined, wringing his hands. "But my job is to take these thieves and criminals to the coast."

Thieves? Criminals? Squaring her shoulders, Danielle lifted her chin and looked Prince Henry straight in the eye. "A servant is not a thief, Your

Highness," she said boldly. "And those who are thieves cannot help themselves."

The prince and his guardsman exchanged looks. "Really?" the prince said. "Well, then, by all means, enlighten us."

Ignoring her fluttering heart, Danielle explained. "If you suffer your people to be ill educated and their manners corrupted from infancy, and then punish them for those crimes to which their first education disposed them, what else is to be concluded, sire, but that you first make thieves and then punish them?"

The prince's mouth twitched slightly, as if he was holding back a smile. "Well, there you have it," he announced to the crowd of onlookers. He turned to the wagon master. "Release him."

The man hesitated. "Sire, my orders are—"

"I said release him!" the prince shouted. Another murmur went up from the crowd at the show of royal emotion.

Scarcely believing that her plan had worked, Danielle watched with silent joy as a group of guards loosed the chains that bound Maurice. As he climbed down from the wagon, his clothes dirty and tattered, his expression was dazed. "I thought I was looking at your mother," he murmured to Danielle, his eyes misty.

"Meet me at the bridge," she said to him

51

quietly. Then, in a voice she knew the nobles who surrounded her would hear, she declared, "We leave at once. See to the carriage."

As Maurice stumbled ahead, his legs and arms stiff from being chained, Danielle faced the prince and curtsied. "I thank you, sire." Turning on her tattered heel, which was hidden beneath the elegant gown, she strode toward the main gate of the castle.

Hurry, hurry, a little voice inside her head warned. *It's not too late for them to realize who you really are.*

Out of the corner of her eye, she saw that the prince was following her. In fact, he was right at her back.

"I could have sworn I knew every courtier in the province," he mused, striding alongside her. "Have we met?"

His gaze was so direct, so curious, that Danielle felt she might faint. Whether it was from fear of being found out, or from fear of being near someone so . . . so beautiful, she didn't know.

"I am visiting a cousin," she managed to say.

"Who?"

"My cousin," Danielle replied, quickening her pace.

"Yes, you said that. Which one?"

He certainly deserved high marks for persistence. "The only one I have, sire." She bit the inside of her lip and hurried forward, her eyes on the immense gates that stood between her and safety.

"Then, please, tell me your cousin's name, so that I might call upon her to learn who you are." His voice softened. "For anyone who can quote Thomas More is well worth the effort."

A slight flush of embarrassment rose in Danielle's cheeks. He had found her out. "The prince has read *Utopia*?" she asked.

The prince nodded, chuckling. "I found it sentimental and dull." He shrugged. "I confess, the plight of the everyday rustic bores me."

Danielle stopped suddenly. Could anyone, even a prince, be so superior? She gestured to the departing prison wagons. "I gather you do not converse with many peasants?" Her blood grew hot.

The prince laughed heartily. "Certainly not! No." He looked at her as if she were mad. "Naturally not."

"Excuse me, sire, but there is nothing natural about it," she retorted. "A country's character is defined by its everyday rustics, as you call them, and their position demands respect. Not . . .

not . . ." She knew she was sputtering, but she couldn't help it. What a sad state of affairs that a person like this, with such backward views, would someday rule all of France!

Prince Henry's face was a mixture of fascination and surprise as he stood opposite her. "Am I to understand you find me arrogant?"

Danielle gave him a look that said exactly that and then some. "You gave one man back his life, but did you even glance at the others?"

There was nothing he could say, Danielle thought smugly. She had him.

The prince stepped closer, staring into her eyes. "Who *are* you?" he whispered.

Suddenly Danielle became aware that a crowd surrounded them. A very quiet, intensely interested crowd. She gulped, her bravado draining out of her faster than water evaporating from a moat on a hot August day.

"I fear the only name to leave you with is . . . Comtesse Nicole de Lancret," she said, scrambling for an answer.

"There now, that wasn't so hard," the prince said with a smile.

A woman's voice rang across the courtyard. "Henry, you're back!"

A beautifully dressed woman, her hair and

face immaculate, glided toward them. Danielle blanched. It was Queen Marie.

"Hello, Mother," the prince greeted her.

As the two began to converse, Danielle slipped quietly away.

Luck had been with her all day. There was no use tempting the fates now by risking a conversation with the queen. Furthermore, what purpose did it serve to debate the problems of the poor with the prince? It wasn't as if she could ever change his mind.

And, although she didn't want to admit it, gazing at that handsome, chiseled face had stirred up feelings inside her she hadn't known she was capable of feeling.

Feelings a poor servant girl like her couldn't risk having for the Prince of France.

For some reason, Henry felt incredibly calm as his mother escorted him down the long hallway that led to the throne room. The conversation he'd had with Nicole de Lancret had been like no other. The comtesse, a total stranger, had dared to disagree with him. How refreshing it was to see someone so unafraid of a prince, who expressed her opinions . . . who said what she meant with no fear.

As Henry and his mother entered the room, his father looked up from a pile of papers and slammed his fist on his writing desk.

"You, sir, are restricted to the grounds!"

Henry couldn't help himself. He laughed. "Are you putting me under house arrest?"

"You are my son and I am the king," Henry's father burst out. "And I will have my way—"

"Or what?" Henry interrupted. "You'll ship me to the Americas like some criminal? All for the sake of your stupid contract?"

His father leaped to his feet. "You are the Prince of France!" he shouted, his face red as an overripe tomato.

"And it is my life!" Henry shot back. All the emotions that had been pent up inside him came rushing forth in that one sentence.

His mother moved between them. "Francis, sit down before you have a stroke," she said, hushing her husband. "Honestly, the two of you . . ." She reached forward and brushed a lock of hair off Henry's brow. "Sweetheart, you have been born to privilege, and with that come specific obligations."

Henry sighed. "Forgive me, Mother, but marriage to a complete stranger never made anyone in this room very happy."

The sound of his father's scepter smacking the

marble floor startled him. "You will marry Gabriella by the next full moon or I will strike at you any way I can!"

"What's it to be, Father?" Henry couldn't resist taunting. "Hot oil or the rack?"

The king paled. "I will simply deny you your crown and live forever."

Henry knew this was the only threat his father considered worth issuing. But it fell on deaf ears. "Good. Agreed," he said simply. "I don't want it."

Turning his back on his anxious mother and furious father, Henry strode from the room.

Danielle was immensely relieved to learn that Maurice had not suffered too greatly in captivity. She would never have forgiven Rodmilla if he had. Not that she forgave her stepmother anyway. Selling Maurice to pay her taxes was unforgivable. But at least Danielle could rest easy now. After she had returned the borrowed dress and jewels to Gustave's studio, she and Maurice had enjoyed a wonderful conversation as they walked back to the manor, reminiscing about the days when Danielle's father was alive, the glory days of the Manoir de Barbarac.

The two of them made their way through a field of wildflowers, the manor in the near distance. Danielle grinned, envisioning the reunion that was about to take place. Louise was bending over, picking vegetables in the back garden, still in the dark regarding her husband's fate.

Then Louise looked up and spotted them. Her Maurice was home! In a moment everyone—Maurice, Louise, Paulette, and Danielle—shared a teary, joyous embrace.

The warmth of her friends' hugs still lingered on her skin as Danielle entered the manor's great room. She was so happy that even the sight of her stepsisters as they sat playing a game of backgammon didn't bother her.

Until she heard Marguerite's nasal singsong: "Somebody's in trouble."

Before she had time to figure out what the obnoxious girl meant, a rough hand grabbed her by the ear, marched her across the room, and hurled her into a chair. The tiny bouquet of wildflowers she had been holding fluttered to the ground. Danielle looked into Rodmilla's infuriated face.

"You stupid, stupid, girl!" Rodmilla shrieked. "You know how important this is to me! To Marguerite! Why, the whole thing makes me sick! It's deceitfulness, Danielle, and I will not have it in my house!"

Danielle reached up to massage her mistreated ear. "What did I do?" she asked, baffled.

"*Think*, Danielle," Marguerite said through

her teeth, obviously enjoying her stepsister's confusion. "Think hard."

How could they have found out about my borrowing the dress? About the words the prince and I had at the castle? Danielle's mind was a jumble of thoughts. Her eyes flicked to Jacqueline.

"The horse," her stepsister mouthed.

Danielle swallowed with relief. They didn't know anything. "Prince Henry stole our horse this morning," she told them.

"Really?" Rodmilla's voice dripped with sarcasm. "Why, then, that would explain why he *returned it this afternoon*!" She stamped her foot. "How dare you let him surprise me like that!"

"I'm sorry," Danielle said, her voice low.

Rodmilla began to pace the room. "Luckily for you, Marguerite turned in a beautiful performance. She and the prince had quite an interlude."

Marguerite fluffed her hair. "I shouldn't be surprised if he drops by again."

Danielle's pulse quickened. *Prince Henry, here?* If he saw her in this house, it would be a catastrophe. She had already managed to fool him once and had lied about her name. But twice?

"Come, come." Rodmilla snapped her fingers in front of Danielle's face. "I must know exactly what was said. The simplest phrase can have a thousand meanings." She bent down to stare directly into her stepdaughter's eyes. "He said you were forceful," she declared. "What did you say?"

"I called him a thief, *madame*," Danielle said. "I did not recognize him."

Letting out a huge sigh of relief, Rodmilla hugged her. "Oh, Danielle, my little country girl. Now you must work extra hard to make sure the manor is spotless. We cannot have the royal bottom sitting on a dirty chaise, now, can we?"

Danielle nodded in mute agreement.

"What is *he* doing here?" Marguerite asked, gesturing peevishly at the doorway. There stood Maurice and Louise, their faces anxious.

"I have worked off your . . . my debt, *madame*," Maurice said. "They told me to go home."

Goose bumps formed on Danielle's arms as she waited for the baroness's reply.

Rodmilla studied him. "Fine," she snapped, tilting her head toward the barnyard. "Go catch a chicken."

Normally the king did not knock when he entered a room. After all, he was the king, and this was his castle. But considering the stature of his guest, decorum dictated that he must knock. Not that it mattered. Leonardo da Vinci was so obsessed with his latest project that he didn't hear the king's polite raps on the door.

Taking the liberty of entering, King Francis walked slowly through the Italian master's bedchamber. He was amazed by the designs and models that cluttered the room. Sketches were propped against the walls, books teetered in disorganized piles, and dirty paintbrushes and charcoals lay in disarray on the floor. The king was impressed . . . obviously he was in the realm of a genius.

"I understand I have you to thank for my son's being home," the king said, his voice breaking the silence. Leonardo said nothing, did not even look up from his project. The king cleared his throat. "These last few years haven't been easy. He's become . . . confused."

Leonardo put aside the sketch he had been working on. "Confused how, sire?"

"He doesn't want to be king." The king's heart filled with despair as he said the words.

"Why not?" Leonardo asked. Picking up a miniature figurine draped with a piece of cloth, he walked past Francis and out onto the castle ramparts.

"I don't know, really," the king said, following. "Something about not wanting to take over the family business, I suppose." The sight before him was majestic: a forest in summer bloom, the deep waters of the moat sparkling in the bright sunshine, dots of color that were workers bustling about the day's tasks on the castle grounds. How could his son turn all this away?

Leonardo threw the figurine off the ledge, and the two men watched it fall like a stone to the walkway below. Leonardo sighed. "My father wanted me to be a lawyer."

"That, *signore*, would have been a tragedy." The king was indignant.

Leonardo's brilliant eyes glittered up at him. "Perhaps your son's calling is a voice only he can hear." Abruptly he walked back into the bedchamber.

Again the king followed, puffing out his chest. "Like a mountain of granite, that boy, but I too am a mountain, and a far more stubborn one."

The artist shrugged. "Then I see no solution, Your Majesty, unless of course, one of you were to become a river."

A river? King Francis watched, fascinated, as Leonardo picked up a piece of material from which hung a small string and, wrapping it around the king's finger, tied it in a knot. "And why would we do that?"

Leonardo removed the knotted string from

the king's finger. "It is just that a river is much stronger than a mountain," he said casually.

"Go on." King Francis was intrigued.

"A river's strength is derived from its fluid nature. Create a dam and it will find a way around it." Leonardo and the king walked onto the ramparts again.

"And this cursed boy," the king muttered, "how do I get around him?"

Leonardo stared out at the wide expanse of nature that lay below them. "May I humbly submit, sire, that if France and Spain wish to fortify their alliance with a contract, let the treaty be between kings, not children. A river changes course, Majesty, but it always finds a way to the sea." He handed the king the material and string. "Throw."

King Francis tossed the bit of cloth into the air. Like magic, a gust of wind swept up the fabric and carried it off.

"The next time I fall from the heavens, remind me to call you," the king said under his breath. As the artist went back to his work, the king began to think. Signore da Vinci's words of advice had been insightful. Maybe there was another solution to his problem.

Saying a quick goodbye to his new friend, the king hurried along the corridor and swooped down the elegant marble staircase that bore his emblem, the fire-breathing salamander. With smooth strides, he left the castle, crossed the courtyard, and passed the manicured gardens. Seconds later he burst into the tree-lined arboretum, where he knew his wife and son would be taking their late-afternoon stroll. Sure enough, they were there, walking arm in arm beneath the ivy-covered trellis, engaged in conversation about some Comtesse de Lancret.

The king interrupted them. "In honor of Signore da Vinci, I have decided to throw a ball. A masked ball. At which point you"—he pointed at his son—"and I will reach a compromise."

"Compromise?" Prince Henry repeated. "You?"

King Francis gave his son his most regal stare. "If love is what you seek, I suggest you find it before then. For five days hence, at the stroke of midnight, you will announce your engagement to the girl of your choice . . . or I will announce it for you. Are we agreed?" He felt immensely proud of himself. There was no way his son could protest that this was unfair.

The prince considered for a moment. "And what of your treaty?"

"Let me worry about Spain," the king advised him. "You've got bigger problems." He took the queen's hand and she squeezed his fingers, giv-

64

ing him a smile that set his middle-aged heart thumping.

"Choose wisely, Henry," Queen Marie told their son. "Divorce is something they only do in England."

Henry nodded. "Thank you, Father."

The king nodded in response and turned to go back indoors. "I am France," he whispered to himself. "I am a river. . . ."

Chapter Four

*R*odmilla held the parchment between her fingers. Her eyes scanned the crisp white paper greedily. An invitation to the royal masque for herself and her daughters. She couldn't have asked for a better gift.

"And the engagement?" she asked sweetly, addressing the royal page who stood waiting for her response in the manor doorway.

"Canceled," he replied, eager to please. "Rumor has it that he must find himself a bride before the night of the masque."

Rodmilla's dark eyes clouded over. "That doesn't give us much time." And she would not waste a single second.

Licking her lips, she took the page's sweaty hand in her own cool one. Slowly and deliberately, she reached into her pocket and pulled out a stash of coins.

"I shall need to know who the competition is," she began, pressing a coin into the page's palm and gazing seductively into his eyes. "Every move he makes," she continued, laying down another coin. "His agenda," she went on, adding yet another coin, "and any other tidbits you can dig up." She shoved the rest of the coins into the page's hand and squeezed so hard that the page flinched.

"He's playing tennis with the Marquis de Limoges tomorrow noon," the flustered man babbled, his face the same red as his tunic.

Rodmilla smiled a sugary smile and caressed his cheek. "A skin of such elegance concealing such ruthlessness." She traced an invisible line from his earlobe to his trembling lips. "I've grown rather fond of our intrigues together. Surely you must know that."

"I have an inkling, milady," he breathed.

"When my daughter is queen, perhaps we can find a new arrangement."

Before the confused man knew what was happening, Rodmilla had steered him out the door.

Giving him a brief, coy smile, she closed the door between them and licked her lips once more.

Victory was almost hers. She could taste it.

Danielle could almost taste the sweet, thick honey, blended into her nightly cup of coffee or spooned onto a piece of day-old bread left over from Rodmilla's last meal. Tending to the bee-hives had frightened her at first, but she liked it now, liked watching the busy bees grow calm as wisps of smoke from her handheld smoker drifted over them. They were calm enough for her to reach into the hive and pull out a honey-comb. Carefully she shook off the handful of bees that lingered on the comb, gently shooing them back into the hive. Then she handed the honey-comb to Paulette, who put it safely in her mesh basket.

Across the way stood Maurice and Louise, hanging up laundry and laughing with one another like giddy schoolchildren.

"You did a wonderful thing yesterday, child. Wonderful." Paulette's eyes were full of admiration.

Danielle moved to the left, delicately waving the smoker. "Makes the whole place feel nicer, doesn't it?"

Paulette let out a deep sigh. "I'd have given

anything to see you all dressed up like a courtier. Speaking to the prince like a lady."

"Scolding him was more like it." Danielle wrinkled her nose. "The man is insufferable."

"Yes, you've been saying that *all* day."

Danielle pouted. "Well, it's as true now as it was this morning."

"But darling, he's royalty," Paulette reminded her. "They're born like that."

"Then I suppose the penalty for being wealthy is that you have to live with the rich."

"I'll bet he's quite charming once you get to know him," Paulette said knowingly.

"Honestly, he and Marguerite deserve each other." Danielle handed the older woman another honeycomb.

"Bite your tongue!" Paulette burst out. "The only throne I want her sitting on is the one I have to clean every day."

Danielle looked at Paulette . . . and the two of them dissolved into laughter.

Friends like this made life as a servant a lot easier.

Sucking in her stomach, Jacqueline managed to fasten the last hook on the bright green gown. She had thought it would fit, but now that it was on, her ribs were beginning to ache.

Best to go show Mother and Marguerite and see what they think. Jacqueline crossed the hall to her sister's room, moving as fast as the tight gown would allow.

Marguerite's lavishly decorated bedroom was a disaster. Armoires were open, empty hangers dangling. Silk undergarments littered the bed, and a gigantic pile of beautiful gowns had been tossed carelessly on the floor. Amid the wreckage stood Jacqueline's mother and sister, scrutinizing one gown after another.

"Oh, my darlings, the years have not been kind, but this just proves that even God is helping us now." Jacqueline knew her mother was talking about the royal masque. There had been no other topic of conversation once the prized invitation had arrived.

Rodmilla held up a dress for Marguerite's inspection. "And what's wrong with this one?"

Jacqueline was eager to find out. The pale flowered satin gown with the high puffy sleeves tapered to the wrist looked perfectly lovely to her.

"It's blue!" Marguerite said vehemently.

"*Henry . . . loves . . . blue,*" Rodmilla said, exaggerating each word.

Marguerite yanked the dress from her mother's hands and flung it on the floor along with the rest.

"And fifty other girls will be wearing the exact same color."

Jacqueline watched as her mother's expression grew proud.

"Very good, Marguerite," Rodmilla said.

"This one is too small," Jacqueline piped up, stepping into the room and pointing to herself. She tried to ignore the biting stabs of pain where the dress was pulled too tight.

"Then we shall get you a tighter cinch," Rodmilla said impatiently, pulling an embroidered yellow cape from the pile.

"I cannot breathe as it is!" Jacqueline blurted out.

Rodmilla put her hands on her hips. "If one cannot breathe, one cannot eat."

Jacqueline's face fell. Her mother was right, but if she could not eat, what point was there in attending the masque? Clearly it was Marguerite's night to shine. Jacqueline would simply be in the background . . . stuffed like a sausage into the green dress.

Marguerite shook a silk petticoat in her mother's face. "Mother. Focus. Please."

Rodmilla looked as if she were at a loss. "Perhaps if I knew what you were looking for?"

"Something fit for a queen!"

Suddenly a light seemed to dawn in Rodmilla's brain. Hurriedly she ushered the two girls down the hall to her room. "Come, ladies, I have just the thing. But we must speak of this to no one."

"Oh, I do love a good intrigue!" Marguerite was gleeful. The sisters huddled around their mother and watched as she unlocked the old cedar chest that stood against the wall. "Waste not, want not," the baroness hummed to herself.

Jacqueline's eyes almost popped out of her head as her mother lifted a beautiful beaded gown from the chest.

"Ah, perfect!" Marguerite squealed.

Jacqueline scooped up a pair of exquisite silver satin slippers that lay buried under the dress. "Where did you get these?" she marveled.

"It's Danielle's dowry. For her wedding," Rodmilla explained, her lip curling into a sneer.

Marguerite snorted. "Cinderella, married? To whom, the chimney sweep?"

"But Mother, if it's *her* gown, perhaps she'll want to wear it to the ball," Jacqueline said timidly.

"Since when does a royal function include commoners?" Marguerite demanded.

"Well . . . since never," Jacqueline admitted.

"But she is our stepsister, and the invitation did say—"

"She is not of noble blood!" Marguerite said hotly, grabbing the dress.

"By rights she can go!" Jacqueline protested. This was too much. How could they paw through Danielle's dowry and plan to use these precious things themselves?

"Yes, and who would notice?" Rodmilla asked. "No one!"

Marguerite shook her head in disgust. "Honestly, Jacqueline. Whose side are you on?"

Jacqueline was so angry that she was just about to tell her when a voice startled them all.

"What are you doing?" There in the doorway stood Danielle, her arms weighed down with logs for the fire.

"Well, what does it look like?" Rodmilla said smoothly. "I am airing out your dress for the masque."

"Her dress?" Jacqueline's brow furrowed. "But you just said—"

Marguerite shot her sister an evil look, and Jacqueline immediately fell silent. Had she misunderstood the whole scene? Had she said the wrong thing?

"I suppose for a commoner it will have to do."

Marguerite gave the fabric a disdainful flick with her nail as she handed it back to Rodmilla. "I mean, look at it—it's practically an antique."

"You wish me to go to a ball?" Danielle asked, obviously overwhelmed.

"Of course." Rodmilla sounded shocked by the very question.

Jacqueline *was* shocked. Her stepsister had never been included in anything before. *Why now?* Then a chill spread over her as she watched her mother's steely expression form itself into a deceitful smile. This was no different from any other time. Her mother was laying a plot. Danielle would not go to the masque. Rodmilla was just letting her think she would.

"I do not know what to say," Danielle replied shyly. She took a step toward the baroness as if to embrace her.

"Say?" Rodmilla stiffened, and Danielle stood still. "Honestly, Danielle, it hurts me that you don't feel like one of my daughters."

"I only meant—"

"I thought we could all go as one big, happy family." Rodmilla arched an eyebrow. "That is, if you complete your chores in time and mind your manners until then."

Jacqueline dropped the slippers back into the trunk. Danielle could be a saint for the next week

74

and her mother would still find some excuse not to let her go. Nauseated by her family's loathsome behavior, Jacqueline hurried out of the room.

"What's the matter with her?" Danielle asked.

"She doesn't want you to go," Jacqueline heard Marguerite reply.

Jacqueline stormed blindly down the dark hallway, anger welling up inside her. Danielle had always been kind, always hardworking, but it didn't matter. Rodmilla and Marguerite had no intention of letting Danielle get within a hundred feet of the masque.

Jacqueline only wondered how they would stop her.

"Word has it your hunt this morning was canceled," Leonardo commented from where he stood on the riverbank. Beside him sat a wagon, from which he withdrew two wooden contraptions, each several feet long and resembling nothing so much as enormous shoes.

Henry nodded and skipped another stone across the cool, dark water. "I've never seen so many women out for a walk. Somebody could have been killed."

Leonardo gave him a wry smile. "Or married."

Henry had wandered down to the riverbank to kill time . . . and to think. He was restless these days. Pleasing himself or pleasing his parents . . . which would it be? His father had been generous to give him a chance to select his own bride, but if he couldn't find someone, what would he be left with?

"Do you really think there is only one perfect mate?" he asked the artist.

"As a matter of fact, I do."

Henry ran his fingers distractedly through his hair. "Then how can you be certain to find her? And if you do find her, is she really the one for you, or do you only think she is?" He flung another stone into the water. "And what happens if the person you are supposed to be with never appears . . . or she does but you're too distracted to notice?"

Leonardo gazed off into the distance. "You learn to pay attention."

"Fair enough," Henry agreed. "So let's say God puts two people on earth and they're lucky enough to find one another. But one of them gets hit by lightning. Then what? Is that it? Or, perchance, say you meet someone new and marry all over again. Is that the lady you were supposed to be with? Or was it the first?" He knew he was rambling, but he couldn't stop. "And if so, when the two of them were walking side by side, were they both the one for you and you just happened to meet the first one first? Or was the second one supposed to be first? How does a person know how things are meant to be?"

Leonardo toyed with the shoelike contraptions. "You cannot leave everything to Fate, boy. She's got a lot to do. Sometimes you must give her a hand."

Henry supposed he was right. Automatically his thoughts turned to the beautiful Comtesse Nicole de Lancret. He'd definitely be willing to give Fate a hand where she was concerned. If only he could see her again. Then he could settle the question that had been plaguing his every waking moment . . . had he met his soul mate?

Heavens, it's hot. Danielle removed the floppy old work hat she wore during the summer and wiped the sweat from her brow. She and Petit-Four, the manor's resident pig, had been digging in the local fields for truffles since sunup. Petit-Four had the best snout around. No truffle was safe with her on the trail.

Longingly Danielle thought of the river. How delicious it would be to cool her steaming skin and blistered toes in the water. Not only would it be a treat, it was a necessity, she decided as she stared down at her filthy dress and arms. She couldn't go home looking like a pig herself. Her mind made up, Danielle ran through the field to where the river beckoned below.

After stripping down to her undergarments, Danielle dove expertly into the water, allowing the Loire to sweep her up and carry her away. After a few moments of splashing about, she floated on her back and stared dreamily at the clouds, relishing her solitude. It was wonderful to relax, dreaming of a world where truffles grew on logs, where sunny days were spent reading books under trees, where families were filled with love and kind words . . .

"Lovely day."

"*Ahhh!*" Danielle screamed, and then she began to sputter, her arms flailing wildly and her mouth filling with river water. An elderly gentleman, fully dressed and wearing enormous pontoonlike wooden shoes, was walking across the water! Apparently the man was just as frightened as she was, for when she screamed, he lost his balance and fell headfirst into the river.

A second later, the two huge shoes—minus their owner—bobbed to the surface beside her.

Coughing and sputtering, Danielle grabbed a shoe. The old man popped to the surface and grabbed the other. Together they paddled toward the riverbank.

A tall young man stood there waiting. "Signore da Vinci, are you all right?" he asked the old man, splashing through the shallow water to help him.

"I should leave walking on water to the son of God," da Vinci said, wringing the water from his shirt. "Fortunately, I tripped over an angel." He smiled at Danielle.

Smiling weakly, Danielle locked eyes with the young man . . . and felt her stomach lurch.

"Comtesse?" Prince Henry asked, dumbstruck.

"Y-Your Highness?" Danielle stammered. She flung her wet body on the ground. *Oops, wait a minute. I'm supposed to be a courtier. I'm supposed to be regal!* With all the dignity she could muster, she stood up again, trying to ignore the slimy river mud and clumps of grass that stuck to her skin. "Careful, it's very slippery right there," she said airily.

"Here, please, allow me," Henry said gently, taking off his cloak and offering it to her.

Only then did Danielle realize that the moment when she'd flung herself prostrate in the mud was not to be her most embarrassing one.

Standing in front of Prince Henry and Leonardo da Vinci in her wet undergarments was about the most humiliating thing she could have done.

But the prince could not have been more gallant. After wrapping the cloak around her shivering shoulders, Henry guided her up the riverbank to a dry patch of ground. There the two of them sat, the sun warming their damp bodies. To their left, Signore da Vinci dug through his wagonload of inventions.

"Where are your attendants?" Henry asked companionably.

Good question. "I . . . um, decided to give them the day off," Danielle answered.

Henry laughed. "A day off? From what, life?"

Danielle answered loftily, "There are days when I wish for nothing more than to be alone."

"Tell me, Nicole de Lancret, why do I get the feeling you're hiding something?" The prince stared intently at her, his face only inches from hers.

Danielle shifted uncomfortably. "I think perhaps you are looking too closely."

Abashed, the prince backed off. "Perhaps I am. I'm afraid, *mademoiselle,* you are a walking contradiction, and I find that rather fascinating."

"Me?" Danielle blinked. Someone like him found someone like her fascinating?

"Yes, you." Henry leaned against her shoulder.

"You spout the ideals of a Utopian society and the abolition of the class system, and yet you live the life of a courtier."

Danielle felt a flutter in her heart. He was so handsome, so charming . . . so . . . *so rich and out of touch,* she reminded herself. "And you own all the land there is, yet take no pride in working it. Is that not also a contradiction?" she asked.

Prince Henry pushed his underlip out, trying to look stubborn. "First I'm arrogant, and now I have no pride. However do I manage that?" His eyes twinkled at her.

"You have everything, and still the world holds no joy," she answered earnestly.

He pulled a blade of grass from the ground and twisted it between his fingers. "How do you do it, then?"

For a moment Danielle wondered what those fingers would feel like intertwined with hers . . . "Do what?" she asked abruptly.

"Live each day with this kind of passion." Prince Henry leaned back on his elbows. "Don't you find it exhausting?"

"Only when I am around you," Danielle replied teasingly. "Why do you like to irritate me so?"

A grin formed on his lush, full lips. "Why do *you* rise to the bait?"

Danielle was just about to answer him when a woman's voice beckoned from across the river-bank. *"Danielle? Danielle!"*

Scrambling to her feet, Danielle saw Jacqueline, pig in tow, her hand shading her eyes from the sun. Jacqueline was obviously looking for her . . . and if she found her, there would be some serious explaining to do.

"You will have to excuse me, Your Highness. I have lost track of the hour," Danielle said hurriedly.

"But the wind." Leonardo came over to them, holding an elaborate creation of paper and wood in his arms. "It is perfect."

"I'm sorry," Danielle said, beads of sweat breaking out on her forehead. Nothing would have suited her better than to linger in the company of the wise old artist and the prince, but it was impossible.

"I'm playing tennis tomorrow with the Marquis de Limoges," the prince said, his voice eager. "Will you come?"

Danielle shot one last look at Jacqueline. She and Petit-Four were getting closer. "I really must go." With a brief, apologetic smile, she took off the cloak, threw it at the prince, and raced up the hill. As she ran, only one thought coursed through her mind: How had she suddenly changed from a working-class girl to a courtier, keeping company with France's future king?

I don't know, she thought with a smile. She scooped her clothes off the ground and tore through the field toward home. *But my life has certainly gotten a lot more interesting.*

Chapter Five

"**P**aulette, where are the candlesticks?" Rodmilla squinted in the nearly black dining room. "We can hardly see our plates."

"They are missing, milady," Paulette replied. "I have searched high and low."

Danielle stood alongside Louise and Paulette at the end of the room, her palm pressed against the smooth crystal water pitcher she was carrying. Lately it seemed that every few days something disappeared. And her stepmother was growing more and more snappish.

Marguerite shot a suspicious look at Louise. "The painting in the upstairs hall is gone too. It seems we have a thief in our midst."

Danielle could feel the two older women

stiffen. Her throat was dry. The fact that things had gone missing was a mystery, but surely none of her friends had anything to do with it.

Rodmilla plunked down her fork. "So this is how I am treated after all our years together. My husband's prized possessions . . . *gone*." She narrowed her eyes, eyes that had grown beadier each year that Danielle had had to look at them. "Well, I shall garnish all your wages until the pilfered items are returned. Is that understood?"

"Yes, *madame*," Paulette, Louise, and Danielle replied. *Even though I'm not paid*, Danielle thought wryly.

Rodmilla picked up a platter of meat. "Perhaps I should ship you all off to the Americas with the rest of the thieves."

"Oh, didn't you hear?" Jacqueline asked excitedly. "The prince went to the king and asked him to release all those men."

"He didn't!" Danielle exclaimed, clutching the pitcher to her chest.

Rodmilla glared at her. Danielle blushed. As a servant, she was supposed to pretend not to hear the conversation that took place at the dinner table, but it was rather difficult. Especially when it involved something as amazing as the prince's releasing the prisoners!

"By royal decree, any man who sails must now

be compensated," Jacqueline finished, reaching for a thick slice of bread.

"Compensated?" Rodmilla shook her head. "Honestly, what is this world coming to?"

Marguerite leaned forward, her elbows on the dining room table. "Well, what I want to know is, who is this comtesse everyone is talking about? Why, there must've been ten courtiers speaking of her today and how the prince fell all over himself about her." She tapped her water goblet, and Danielle stepped forward and filled it.

"We will find out who she is and bury her," Rodmilla vowed.

Danielle's hand shook so much she was surprised she could keep from spilling the water. She knew how badly her stepmother was determined to marry her older daughter off to the prince, but even Danielle was astonished by the viciousness in her voice at the slightest hint that Marguerite might have competition.

The fact that Danielle herself was the competition didn't make her heart beat more calmly.

"Mother!" Jacqueline exclaimed, shocked too at Rodmilla's angry tone.

"The social pyramid has slippery slopes, Jacqueline." Rodmilla's face was unsympathetic. "Mind you don't fall off."

"It's blasphemy—" Jacqueline began.

"Darling, hell couldn't possibly be worse than a house in the country." Rodmilla put a delicate piece of truffle into her mouth. "These are magnificent. Danielle, thank you."

Danielle nodded, thinking of the companion she'd had after she'd collected those truffles.

He had been rather magnificent too.

Henry smiled with gritted teeth as Pierre le Pieu carefully placed a helmet on his head. *Will we ever be done?* he wondered miserably. He shot a despairing glance at Captain Laurent and a few of his soldier friends. They'd been in the throne room for hours, and Henry had suffered through endless fittings and adjustments as le Pieu, the court armorer, put the final touches on his new suit of armor. The man knew his armor, but Henry found him utterly distasteful. His breath was bad, his teeth were crooked, and he had a way of hovering that made Henry more than a little uncomfortable.

"Begging your pardon, sire," le Pieu wheezed as the metal helmet scraped the exact spot on Henry's brow where the servant girl's apples had hit their mark.

Henry winced. "It's this silly bruise."

"And from a servant, no less," Captain Laurent reminded him.

"I like a woman who hits back," le Pieu said, his thin lips drawn up in a bawdy grin.

Henry raised his eyebrows—not an easy task with the tight-fitting helmet. "Perhaps that explains why you are unwed, sir."

"But I never lack for company," le Pieu confided, slowly circling the prince.

"Company that is bought and paid for, you slimy bastard," Captain Laurent said tersely. It was common knowledge that le Pieu, while not the most attractive middle-aged bachelor in the kingdom, was one of the richest. His money seemed to attract a steady supply of ladies, not all of them reputable.

Le Pieu was unruffled. "We all pay inevitably, Captain. For some of us, it is up front."

A few of the soldiers laughed. Henry used the break in the conversation to draw out his sword. He and Laurent began to duel playfully.

"And what of love, *monsieur*?" Henry said to le Pieu, savoring the sound of metal as his rapier sliced through the air. *Slash.* "Is your soul so satisfied that you can live without it?"

"I am a homely man, sire. I take what I can get."

"Surely there is someone," Henry persisted

teasingly as Laurent's sword crossed his. "A face that keeps you awake at night?"

"There is . . . someone, Your Highness. A commoner," the armorer replied, rubbing his hands together.

"A commoner?" Henry's concentration lapsed for a second, and Laurent quickly scored a jab. "Ow!" Henry rubbed his armor-clad shoulder, pretending to be wounded. "Le Pieu, I'm surprised at you. A commoner?"

Le Pieu shrugged. "Yet I find her spirit intoxicating."

"Intoxicating." Henry mulled over the word. He'd had a few intoxicating experiences himself during the past week. "Well said."

Laurent rolled his eyes. "Do not get him started, le Pieu. We will never hear the end of the Comtesse de Lancret."

"De Lancret?" le Pieu repeated. "That name is unfamiliar to me."

"Yes," Henry replied dejectedly. "To everyone." He'd made inquiries all over the kingdom, but the beautiful Comtesse de Lancret was a complete mystery. He was starting to believe he'd imagined her.

But could he then be imagining the racing of his pulse, or the trembling in his heart every time he thought of her?

No, he'd decided. He could not.

Those were the truest feelings he'd ever felt.

Marguerite cooled her face with a small paper fan. Sitting in the sports arena on a warm summer day watching a tennis match certainly wasn't her idea of a good time . . . except when the players were the Marquis de Limoges and Prince Henry.

That made her suffering much more palatable.

Unfortunately, a lot of other women felt the same way. Marguerite's eyes roamed the seating area. Everywhere she looked, beautiful girls sat alongside their anxious mothers.

"Mother, look how pretty Lulu du Pres has become," Marguerite whispered, staring at the tall redhead in the elegant silk dress.

"She has developed quite nicely, hasn't she?" Rodmilla said grudgingly.

Marguerite looked down at her dress, smoothing the skirt. "But certainly she's not prettier than me," she said fretfully. She bit her lip. "Is she?"

Her mother wasn't listening. Instead she was engaged in a conversation with Celeste and Isabelle. *Those two gadflies are everywhere we go!* Marguerite thought, annoyed.

"My daughters and I were just commenting

on how breathtaking Lulu du Pres has become," Rodmilla confided, raising her voice.

Isabelle nodded. "As were we, Baroness."

"She is a vision," Celeste put in.

"And what a blessing that those horrible pustules haven't yet spread to her face," Rodmilla remarked. "*Tsk, tsk.*"

Marguerite watched as the smiles disappeared from the two courtiers' faces. *Mother is so smart!* she marveled, staring up at Rodmilla with nothing but pure adoration in her eyes.

Her mother was definitely someone to learn from.

Danielle inhaled the early-morning air deeply. She loved market day. Loading up the wagon with apples and grapes and driving into the village wasn't easy, but it was a change of scenery, a change of pace. Anything anyone could want could be found in the village square: choice cuts of meat, fresh eggs and milk, delicious cheeses wrapped in cotton cloths. Not to mention the barbers who tried to entice passersby to have a haircut, the dentists who performed tooth extractions, and the puppeteers who put on delightful shows.

Carefully Danielle arranged the produce in

the back of the wagon. Appearance was important. The more attractive their fruits and vegetables were, the more likely they'd be purchased and served at someone's table that night.

"There I was, prattling on about injustice, while he was actually doing something about it," Danielle told Louise. Ever since she had heard about the prince's granting freedom to the prisoners, her mind had been racing. Had her words influenced him that greatly? *They were my words . . . but it was not I who delivered them. It was the Comtesse de Lancret.* A knot of confusion formed in her gut at the memory.

"Maybe you inspired him," Louise suggested, popping a grape into her mouth.

"If it was me on that riverbank, I would have kept my mouth shut and my options open," Paulette teased.

"I am never going to be that woman again," Danielle said quietly.

"Why, darling?" Paulette's eyes were wide with mock surprise. "You were doing so well. A few more days and we would have had a revolution on our hands."

Danielle stared miserably at her feet in their tattered shoes.

Louise punched Paulette in the arm. "Oh,

hush up, you bag of bones, can't you see she feels bad enough as it is?"

"I'm teasing, you old snail," Paulette retorted. "If it went as bad as she thinks, why would he invite her to tennis?"

"You mean the comtesse," Danielle pointed out glumly.

Paulette tweaked Danielle's cheek. "I mean *you.*"

With a sigh, Danielle finished helping an old peasant woman interested in purchasing some apples. *Who am I? Danielle the servant or Nicole the comtesse?* She threw a rotten apple off the wagon, her expression fierce. *Or am I someone else altogether?*

"Danielle de Barbarac, you get prettier every week."

Danielle dropped the cluster of grapes she was holding. She'd have known that voice anywhere. The nasal twang belonged to Pierre le Pieu, one of the village's most disgusting bachelors.

And for some reason, he seemed to fancy her.

"And you, Monsieur le Pieu, are wasting your flattery," she replied politely. Luckily she had Paulette and Louise with her. The two women crowded around her protectively.

"Pity your soil is the best in the province, and yet so poorly tended."

A nervous shiver spread up Danielle's spine. The old goat wasn't talking about the farmland at the manor . . . he was talking about her. The idea of being with him made her want to vomit.

"We have limited resources," Paulette said brusquely.

"Is there anything I can do?" le Pieu inquired.

"Perhaps you should bring it up with the baroness and stick to shopping," Louise advised, taking Danielle firmly by the arm.

Le Pieu sidled close. "I'd rather discuss it with Danielle, if you don't mind." Stretching out a bony finger, he lifted a wayward strand of hair from her face. "I may be twice your age, child, but I am well endowed, as evidenced by my estate. I have always had a soft spot for the less fortunate. You need a wealthy benefactor, and I need a young lady of spirit. . . ." His voice trailed off.

Danielle rummaged through the wagon and came up with just the right piece of fruit to offer him. "Prunes?"

Le Pieu's smile turned sour. "No, I'll buy nothing this week." He eyed Danielle. "I'd be careful if I were you. Without my generosity, your pathetic farm would cease to exist."

Danielle watched as the haughty fleck of a man drifted off through the crowded marketplace, his parting words sending up warning flags in her mind.

What on earth could le Pieu mean? How had he ever been generous to her?

Henry hadn't meant anything serious by it—just a little walk through the market with him and the royal guard—but Marguerite was acting as if he'd offered her a crown of diamonds on a silver platter. Earlier that day she'd caught his tennis ball at the arena. When he'd gone to retrieve it, he'd been struck by her rather attractive appearance . . . and the fact that her very voluptuous bosom was practically bursting out of a very low-cut gown.

She was no Comtesse de Lancret, though, that was for sure.

But who is? a snide little voice whispered in his ear. *You don't know if you'll ever see her again. You don't even know if she exists, and you have to find a wife soon or your bride will be your father's choice. . . .*

And here was the lovely Marguerite . . . hanging on his every word.

He decided to make the best of it.

"Here," he said, offering her a piece of candy from one of his servants' trays. "Never have you tasted anything so delicious."

Marguerite stopped dead in the street, closed her eyes, and opened her mouth wide.

Slightly embarrassed, Henry laid a tiny piece on her tongue.

"Like it?" he asked.

"Like it?" Her eyes popped open. "Why, it's positively sinful!" she exclaimed rapturously. "What is it called?"

"Chocolate. The Spanish monks keep sending bricks of it. Would you care for another?"

Marguerite eagerly closed her eyes and opened her lustful mouth.

"I, um, think we can do it with our eyes open," Henry said under his breath.

Marguerite leered at him. "But then I'd miss the anticipation."

Rather than argue, he placed another piece of chocolate in her mouth. Ignoring her little moans of delight, he glanced at two older women selling chickens. Their clothes were worn and faded, their hands wrinkled, but they were laughing and talking as if they were the richest women in the kingdom. Behind them was a coop full of birds, and a third woman tending to them, her face obscured by the metal cage.

He thought for a minute. "Marguerite, do you find me arrogant?" he asked suddenly.

"No, Your Highness," Marguerite assured him. "And anyone who does doesn't know you at all."

The prince sighed. "Well, someone told me that our peasantry defines this country's character."

"They were joking, certainly," Marguerite said, simpering.

The comtesse's eyes had been so serious, her speech so direct . . . "No, they weren't." He tilted his head toward the two women. "Shall we go see?" They strolled over to the women's wagon.

As the Prince and Marguerite drew near, Louise and Paulette stared with growing anxiety. Danielle, hidden behind the chicken coop, couldn't see the prince coming. Louise tapped her on the back and Danielle turned, a squirming chicken clutched in her hand. And there he was! *The prince!* Danielle's eyes went wide with horror.

Before he could see her face, Danielle screamed and tossed the squawking bird straight at him. Feathers flew everywhere. The coopful of chickens went mad, squawking and flapping their wings.

The royal guard began shouting and waving their weapons.

While the prince batted the chicken away from his face, Louise and Paulette hid Danielle under the wagon, and the two women ran back and forth, their skirts flapping.

Marguerite looked close to tears. Clusters of feathers stuck to her exposed chest.

Then the dust settled. Henry rubbed his eyes. Louise and Paulette smiled innocently at him, each holding a chicken in her hands. The royal guard scratched their heads in confusion. Marguerite had popped another chocolate into her mouth and brushed away the last of the feathers.

Rodmilla rushed over. "What are you trying to do?" she shrieked at Louise and Paulette. "Scare the prince to death?"

"We was startled is all!" Paulette protested.

Henry looked at the two servants. "Were there just the two of you?"

Louise nodded. "And the, uh . . . chicken, Your Highness."

"It's the oddest thing," he murmured. He'd bet a thousand francs another woman had been with them.

Vanishing women. That was happening a lot lately.

"And then he said the most wonderful thing," Marguerite gushed from the chair beside the water basin. "He said, 'I have no doubt I'll be seeing you at the masque.' Just like that. Why, I practically floated home."

Danielle slid the cake of soap through Rodmilla's oily black hair, working up a thick lather. Years of experience had taught her to be vigorous yet gentle, and she made sure to massage her stepmother's scalp, being careful to use her fingertips, not her nails—although all this talk of the prince and the masque was making her feel quite uneasy.

"Honestly, Mother, *I* caught the tennis ball, and *she* got all the chocolate," Jacqueline said sulkily.

"I am proud of both my girls," Rodmilla declared. "Now we must get our beauty sleep. The prince always attends the eight o'clock mass."

Danielle moved aside as her stepsisters kissed Rodmilla on the cheek, then left the room. She retrieved a pitcher of lukewarm water and poured it slowly over Rodmilla's hair.

"We must push for a quick engagement," Rodmilla thought aloud. "Oh, Paris at Christmas! Can you imagine?" She looked up at Danielle. "No, I don't suppose you can."

Danielle stared down at the woman who sat in the chair below her . . . a woman she barely knew, let alone understood.

"What are you looking at?" Rodmilla snapped.

"Nothing, *madame*." Danielle quickly finished rinsing her hair and began squeezing out the water.

"Well, stop it," Rodmilla told her. "It's not polite to stare. You had better learn some manners."

"Yes, *madame*."

Rodmilla sat up, and after patting her wet head with a towel, Danielle began to comb through her long locks.

"My mother was hard on me too, you know," Rodmilla said, a bit more subdued. "She taught me that cleanliness was next to godliness. She washed my face twenty times a day, convinced it was not clean enough. But I was very grateful. She wanted me to be the best I could be." She sighed, content. "And here I am a baroness . . . and Marguerite shall be queen."

"She is so much like you," Danielle said, sliding the comb down to the ends of Rodmilla's hair.

"Do you really think so?"

"I've heard the courtiers speak of you in town, and—"

"What do they know?" Rodmilla cried, startling her. "They know nothing! It's just talk and malicious gossip!" She paused. "What did they say?"

"They marvel at your beauty," Danielle answered.

"Oh." Rodmilla turned up her nose. "Well. They're just being polite."

Abruptly Rodmilla stood up and directed Danielle into the chair, spinning her to face the gilded mirror on the bedchamber wall.

She lifted a piece of Danielle's hair and let it fall. "Pity you never knew your mother. I'm sure there's a bit of her in you somewhere."

Inside, Danielle's heart was churning. She rarely spoke of her mother . . . the thought of what could have been was too painful. Her mother had died the moment Danielle drew her first breath, and, through no fault of her own, her daughter had spent her childhood and teenage years in a lonely sea of doubts and insecurities.

"I wish I knew what she looked like," Danielle whispered, tears filling her eyes. She lowered her gaze, but Rodmilla's firm finger lifted her chin.

"We must never feel sorry for ourselves. No matter how bad it gets, it can always get worse."

Danielle nodded. "Yes, *madame*."

"You have got so much of your father in you," Rodmilla said. "Sometimes I can actually see him looking out through your eyes."

"Really?" Danielle smiled through her tears.

Rodmilla studied her. "Your features are so

masculine," she lamented. "And then to be raised by a man. It's no wonder you were built for hard labor."

"Did you love my father?" Danielle ventured. She'd never asked her stepmother such a personal question.

It was a mistake.

Rodmilla's face grew cold. "I barely knew him," she replied icily. "Now go away. I'm tired."

Danielle backed out of the room. An act of kindness from her stepmother had been too much to hope for.

She wouldn't make that mistake again.

Chapter Six

*D*anielle zigzagged in and out of the haystacks, her long hair streaming behind her. Signore da Vinci's invention was the most incredible thing she'd ever seen.

A kite, he'd called it, handing the wooden spool wrapped with thread to her. The thread was attached to a wooden cross, which held a large piece of painted paper that looked like two triangles taped end to end. She hadn't let the kite out of her sight since; she loved how it felt to let it soar up into the air. She let the kite fly along in the soft summer breeze, and then she reeled it in a bit.

"My stepmother expects a quick engagement

between Marguerite and the prince," she told Gustave.

Gustave sat nearby hunched over a canvas, painstakingly painting the royal castle, which loomed in the distance. "And what does that mean to you?"

Danielle stood by him. "Well, I suppose then they would all move into the palace and I could stay with the manor," she pointed out. "Turn things around. That's all that matters." Having Rodmilla and the girls out of the manor would be a dream come true. She almost didn't dare dream it.

Gustave wagged his paintbrush at her. "You like him, admit it."

"No." The kite sailed merrily along, a splash of color in the bright blue sky.

"I suppose if you saw him again, you'd simply—"

"Walk right up to him and say, 'Your Highness, my family is *your* family. Please take them away." She curtsied.

"Well, here comes your big chance, because he's headed this way."

Danielle paled. Spinning on her heel, she saw Prince Henry galloping across the fields toward them, the royal coach waiting back on the road.

She reeled in the kite, tossed it on the ground, then dove headfirst behind a haystack.

"I'm looking for Signore da Vinci," the prince told Gustave. "We're to go to the monastery together. Have you seen him?"

"Da Vinci?" Gustave pretended not to know what the prince was talking about.

Danielle peeked out from behind the haystack with one eye.

The prince gestured impatiently to the kite at Gustave's feet. "Isn't that his flying contraption? Where did you get it?"

"From, uh, the Comtesse de Lancret," Gustave said. "She is a friend of his."

Prince Henry grabbed his forearm. "You know her? Please, I must find her. Where is she staying?"

Danielle felt as if she might faint.

"I believe, Your Highness, she is staying with a cousin . . . the, uh, Baroness Rodmilla de Ghent."

Henry chewed his lip. "Mmmm. That does present a problem."

Frantic, Danielle darted from her hiding spot, mouthing, "Shut up!" to Gustave as he looked her way, panic-stricken. Then she darted behind another haystack. He was going to ruin everything!

"But I happen to know she is there, alone,

by herself, at this very moment," Gustave said helpfully.

"Excellent." The prince looked from Gustave's paint-covered smock to his painting. "That's nice." With a quick nod, he galloped away.

Danielle burst out from behind the haystack. "Gustave, you horrible little snipe!"

But Gustave had a dreamy expression plastered on his face. "Did you hear? He liked my work!"

Danielle grabbed him by the shoulders. "And he is headed toward my house!"

He grinned back. "Then I suggest you run."

All at once her panic shifted into excitement.

Maybe Gustave had the right idea.

She raced off.

Danielle splashed through streams. She ran through fields of wheat. She sprinted down the dusty lane that led to the manor. Whether it was Fortune smiling on her or just plain old-fashioned luck, she managed to get inside the kitchen and shut the door just as the prince came galloping up to the Manoir de Barbarac.

When Paulette opened the door a minute later, Danielle was ready, having quickly changed into an embroidered blue gown that Marguerite had discarded months ago.

"Your Highness, what an unexpected surprise." Danielle reached up to adjust her jeweled headband and smooth her freshly coiffed hair, praying that no burrs or leaves remained in it.

The prince leaned against the doorjamb, a roguish grin on his face. "Do you not attend church?"

"My faith is better served away from the rabid crowds," she said demurely.

His mouth twitched. "I'm afraid my father's edict has created quite a stir."

"As did your own when you freed those people. Why didn't you tell me?" she asked.

Henry smiled. "Because you were digging such a lovely hole around yourself."

She smiled back. "I have been forced to re-evaluate you, you know."

"The Franciscans have an astonishing library. Since you are so fond of reading, I thought perhaps you might join me."

Danielle's pulse quickened. Of course she'd heard of the cliffside monastery, but she'd never thought of actually going there. "It's not fair, sire. You have found my weakness, but I have yet to learn yours."

The prince's dark eyes grew soft. "I should think it was quite obvious."

A slow flush spread over her cheeks at the compliment.

A moment of silence passed, and then the royal coach, along with an important-looking guardsman, arrived at the manor's door.

"Captain Laurent, I shall not be needing my horse or your services," the prince called to the guardsman. He offered his hand to Danielle. "Today I am simply . . . Henry."

Barely believing what was happening, Danielle placed her hand in his.

If it didn't sound so insane, she'd have sworn she was falling in love.

Rodmilla had said a thousand silent thankyous when the royal page had stopped her carriage outside the cathedral before mass. When he'd pressed the handkerchief-wrapped object into her hand and whispered what it was, she'd almost kissed his pimply face.

Now that mass was over, she forced her way to the king and queen's royal carriage, dragging her daughters behind her. Shoving a smelly beggar out of the way, she shook open the handkerchief and surreptitiously gave its contents—a delicate gold locket—to Marguerite.

"Make haste, Marguerite, it's now or never."

Sensing her mother's urgency, Marguerite clamped her fingers over the necklace and intercepted the queen.

"Forgive me, Your Majesty, but I believe you dropped this on your way out." She presented the locket.

Queen Marie felt around her neck. "My goodness, I do not even remember putting it on. Thank you, child. I must say, it is a rare person indeed who would return such a priceless keepsake."

Marguerite bowed as low as was humanly possible. "You are too magnanimous, Majesty."

Rodmilla watched with bated breath as the king and queen traded looks and the king gave a nod of approval. The queen's lady-in-waiting whispered Marguerite's name in the queen's ear.

"Marguerite." The queen smiled at her. "We shall have a chat tomorrow, you and I. Bring your mother."

Marguerite cast her eyes down modestly. "As you wish."

Rodmilla tucked the empty handkerchief into her purse. *We're almost there, darlings. . . .*

Henry walked at ease through the mahogany-paneled room. The monastery was like a second home to him, with its thousands of books and tables occupied by silent, meticulous Franciscan monks, all painstakingly transcribing ancient volumes.

He watched, pleased, as the woman he knew as Nicole walked slowly down the aisles, her fingers lingering on each shelf.

"Pick one," he encouraged her.

Danielle shook her head. "I could no sooner choose a favorite star in the heavens."

"What is it that touches you so?" he asked, unable to take his eyes off her. Her skin was glowing, and her eyes shone brighter than any star in the sky.

"I guess it's because when I was young, my father would stay up late and read to me," she recalled. "He was addicted to the written word, and I fell asleep listening to his voice."

"What sort of books?" Henry asked.

"Science. Philosophy." Danielle shrugged. "I suppose they remind me of him. He died when I was eight. *Utopia* was the last book he brought home."

"Which explains why you quote it." Henry's heart went out to the young woman who had lost her father, who had so obviously been molded by his guidance.

Danielle ran her hand over a row of books. "I would rather hear his voice again than any sound in the world."

Henry considered this, then walked toward the stairway.

"Is something wrong?" she asked, following him.

"In all my years of study, not one tutor has ever demonstrated the passion you have shown me in the last two days. You have more conviction in one memory than I have in my entire being."

She gaped at him. "That's not true!"

"Who do you think released those people headed for the Americas?" he asked.

"You did." Her beautiful eyes were troubled.

"No, it was you!" he exclaimed. "I never would have seen them without your eyes. Which is why I couldn't tell you at the river . . . I was ashamed."

Danielle touched his arm. "Your Highness, if there is anything I've said or done that—"

Henry brushed her off. "Please don't. It's not you."

Danielle grinned back at him. "You're right." And then she walked out of the building, leaving Henry chuckling in her wake.

This was quite a woman—one he was glad to have on his side.

Especially today

Because half an hour later, when a wheel of his coach broke on the road outside Dordogne, she was the only one who offered any reasonable solution.

Henry was terribly embarrassed. The drivers and footmen offered to take the carriage back to the monastery for repair. He was about to ask how that would help when Danielle nodded her approval. "That's fine. We shall continue on foot."

"But it's a half a day's walk, Comtesse!" Henry protested. A comtesse to go on foot in the country? He'd never seen it!

"Honestly, Henry," Danielle chided playfully. "Where's your sense of adventure?"

Jacqueline's arms were folded tightly across her chest as their carriage drove through the manor's gate and to the front door.

And they remained folded as she disembarked.

"Now, we mustn't get overconfident, ladies," Rodmilla was saying. "The prince wasn't in church today, and we need to know why."

As Marguerite shoved past her, Jacqueline stamped her foot. "Marguerite gets to do everything!"

"Oh, don't be daft, Jacqueline," her sister snapped. "The queen doesn't even know you exist."

"What Marguerite does is for all of us, darling," Rodmilla said soothingly. "I am counting on you to help her get ready."

"Lovely," Jacqueline grumbled. "Next thing

you know I shall be cleaning the fireplace with Danielle."

"Where *is* that girl?" Rodmilla asked, looking around.

"Probably off catching rabbits with her teeth," Marguerite said, giggling at her little joke.

Paulette greeted them at the door. "Begging your pardon, milady, but the gilded mirror in your bedchamber. Did you move it?"

"Of course not, why?" Rodmilla asked.

"It's missing." Paulette's face was ashen.

Rodmilla waved her hand in the air. "Then it too shall come out of your pay."

They might not have been her friends, but Jacqueline knew that Paulette and Louise would not steal anything belonging to the manor.

But if not the servants, then who?

Henry scratched his head, carefully avoiding Danielle's eyes. "You would think I would know the way to my own castle."

Why is it men never stop for directions? Danielle thought irritably as she took off her dress and shoes, tossed them aside, and scampered up the cliff. Not that she wasn't enjoying her day with the prince, but she had to get home. She scanned the countryside. "Ah, there it is! It's back that way," she called down to him.

Henry turned. "And I still can't believe that I'm down here while you're up there. And in your undergarments, no less!"

Danielle raised her eyebrows. "I couldn't very well climb up here in that gown, now, could I? Besides, you might break your royal neck, and then where would we be?"

"You swim alone, climb rocks, rescue servants." He laughed. "Is there anything you don't do?"

"Fly." She waved him away. "Now turn around so I can climb back down."

She had just found the first crevice in the rock when a shout from below almost made her lose her balance. She had only turned her back for a second, but in the blink of an eye, Henry had been surrounded by twelve men on horseback . . . one of whom had a sword and dagger pointed straight at him. A gang of Gypsy thieves!

Danielle gasped.

"Stay aloft, *madame*!" Henry shouted. "We've got company!"

As swords began to clash, Danielle grabbed a sturdy-looking vine and began to make her way to the bottom of the cliff.

The rascally man who had drawn his sword leered up at Danielle, then lifted her discarded dress with the point of the weapon. "My wife thanks you for this fine garment, *mademoiselle*."

Danielle continued to climb down. "You will give me back my dress, sir," she called out calmly.

"Let the girl go!" Henry cried, motioning to Danielle to stay out of things.

"And leave you here?" she cried. "I should think not."

"There'll be nothing left when I am finished with him!" the swordsman threatened.

"Finished with me?" Henry raised his sword in the air. "Why you ugly, pus-faced toad!" The two men began to fight, the sounds of metal and heavy breathing filling the country air.

When she was only a few feet from the ground, Danielle managed to kick one man squarely in the face, sending him to the ground. She then leaped on the rascal who was attacking Henry. But before she could give him a roundhouse kick, another Gypsy pressed a knife to her throat.

Henry stood, his chest heaving. "Let her go. Your quarrel is with me."

The Gypsy leader nodded to his men. "Release her."

The knife was removed, but Danielle didn't budge. "I insist you return my things at once! And since you deprive me of my escort, I demand a horse as well." She stood tall, her gaze falling on each of the Gypsies.

The Gypsy leader began to laugh. "Milady, you

may have anything you can carry." Soon his whole gang was doubled over with mirth.

"May I have your word on that, sir?" Danielle asked evenly.

"On my honor as a Gypsy. Whatever you can carry."

With sure, firm strides, Danielle walked past her discarded clothes and scooped up the prince. Taking only a second to adjust his weight, she gave the Gypsy leader a short curtsy, then strolled off through the woods.

Not for nothing had she lifted ten buckets of water every day for years.

"Wait!" cried the leader of the Gypsies, his voice muffled by the howls of laughter from his men. "Please, come back! I will give you a horse."

Danielle grinned at the prince, who smiled at her, his face a mixture of amusement and shock. *Damsel in distress? Ha!*

Henry leaned back against the cavern wall and enjoyed the sweet taste of grappa, the Gypsies' unaged brandy. He'd never drink and ride, of course, but the Gypsies had promised to shelter him and Nicole for the night in their cave, so they were free to indulge. Henry stared lovingly at the comtesse, who was plopped on the ground beside him. She was so beautiful, her long hair in disheveled clumps, her face flushed from the heat of the Gypsies' bonfire. . . .

"You are reading my thoughts, milord," Danielle said as he spun a jug of grappa on the cold dirt beneath them.

"And they are as fuzzy as my own, Comtesse." Henry picked up his nearly empty glass, guzzled the dregs, then promptly fell over backward. Danielle fell next to him, giggling wildly.

"You do your kingdom proud, sir," she told him with a laugh.

Henry stared at the ceiling. Everything was so fuzzy all of a sudden. "Oh, my head is spinning," he whispered.

"I have never been so dizzy," Danielle confided, rolling from side to side.

Henry propped himself up on an elbow. "Then here—quit moving." Gently he cradled her face and pulled her toward him.

Their lips met.

Henry had never been so dizzy either.

Dizzy with love.

The next morning came much too soon. Henry could have held the sleeping comtesse in his arms for all eternity. With great reluctance, he had placed her on a Gypsy's horse and guided it back to the comtesse's cousin's house, the

Manoir de Barbarac. They stood there now, outside the gate.

Helping her down from the horse, the prince allowed his hands to remain clasped loosely around her waist. He was glad she didn't brush him away. He knew he was being quite familiar, but after the kisses they had shared last night, he couldn't help feeling especially tender in her presence.

"You saved my life, you know," he told her. "Back there in the woods."

"A girl does what she can, sire," she said, her eyes shining in the early-morning light.

"Henry," the prince corrected her.

"Henry," Danielle repeated softly.

Again they kissed. Her mouth was warm and inviting, and despite the fact that his feet were planted firmly on the ground, Henry felt as if he were floating.

He'd kissed many women before. But none moved his heart as this one did.

They pulled apart, then kissed once more—the lightest of kisses. Danielle flashed him a brilliant smile as she began walking up the drive.

"Nicole?" Henry called out, wanting to prolong their parting in any way he could.

She turned.

"Do you know the ruins at Amboise?" he asked.

"Yes."

"I often go there to be alone. Would you meet me there tomorrow?"

A look he could not read came into her eyes. "I shall try."

"Then I shall wait all day," he promised. He slung himself up on the horse and galloped for home.

Only a few servants were moving about when Henry arrived at the castle. They were surprised to see him up at such an early hour. If any of them wondered whether he had stayed out all night, none dared ask.

Giving them the briefest of nods, he jogged up the stairs and burst into his parents' bedroom. He grabbed the heavy curtains and pulled them aside. Bright sunlight splashed across the floor ... and into his father's eyes.

"Off with his head!" his father muttered, shaking off the last remnants of a dream.

His mother stretched her arms over her head and gave her husband a slight shake. "Wake up, Francis. It appears your son has something to tell us."

That he did. "Mother, Father. I want to build a university. With the largest library on the continent. Where anyone can study, no matter their station." He rocked back on his heels.

The king and queen traded looks.

"All right, who are you and what have you done with our son?" the king demanded, only half joking.

"And I want to invite the Gypsies to the masked ball," Henry continued. Before his parents could reply, he left the room.

"What's the matter with him?" the king's voice boomed down the hallway.

The queen only smiled. "He's in love."

Chapter Seven

*S*lowly she wrapped her arms around his neck, peppering his face with kisses. His silky black hair slipped between her fingers as she whispered, "Henry, I must tell you something. I am not who you think I am. My name is not Nicole. It is Danielle, and I—"

He jabbed her sharply in the ribs. "You lied to me?"

"N-No," she began, rubbing the spot he had poked. "I mean, not intentionally. I—"

He jabbed her again. "I was at your house last night. Where were you?"

The prince had been at the manor? Suddenly everything was melting before her eyes, including Henry's beautiful, chiseled face. "I—"

Another jab, this time in her stomach.

"Where were you?"

Danielle's eyes fluttered open. Rodmilla stood before her, the old wooden broom clutched in her hands. *Now there's a switch. Rodmilla with the broom . . .*

Her stepmother shook it menacingly, threatening to jab her again.

"I got lost," Danielle mumbled as the realization that she'd been dreaming swept over her.

"I don't believe it," Rodmilla snapped. "You are hiding something from me—I can feel it—and I demand to know what it is."

"Then, please, tell me so that I might go back to sleep." Danielle yawned.

"What about our breakfast?" came Marguerite's nasal whine from the doorway.

"You have two hands," Danielle muttered. "Fix it yourself." She curled back up into the warm ball she'd been in several minutes earlier.

Marguerite let out a gasp. "Why, you lazy little leech!"

"Jacqueline, go boil some water," Rodmilla said, calmly accepting her refusal.

"Me, boil water?" Jacqueline shook her head. "Oh, I knew it. I just knew it."

But Danielle didn't hear the complaints flying about—or the odd note of acceptance in her stepmother's voice.

122

She was already asleep . . . and dreaming of the prince.

Late that afternoon, Danielle dragged herself from her bed and out to the well, where she splashed cold water on her puffy face. She'd never felt so tired in her life, but she knew if she didn't get moving, there would be hell to pay.

She was right.

"Mistress, you'd better get in there quick!" Paulette cautioned from an upstairs window, her voice hushed.

What can Rodmilla want now . . . another pot of jam? Kindling for the fire? Whatever it was, she'd have to do it. Quickly wiping her hands on her skirt and blotting her cheeks dry with her sleeve, Danielle walked through the manor until she came to Rodmilla's bedroom. The voices inside were excited but hushed. Danielle pushed open the door. Rodmilla and Jacqueline sat on the bed. Danielle's dowry chest lay open in front of them. In the middle of the room stood Marguerite, holding up Danielle's mother's wedding gown.

"Well, look who finally decided to grace us with her presence," sneered Rodmilla.

Danielle stared at the gown, clutched greedily in Marguerite's hands. "What do you think you are doing?" she asked, her voice strangled.

Marguerite fluffed her hair. "Trying on my dress."

Danielle gasped.

Rodmilla only smirked. "Do you honestly think after that performance this morning that I'd let you go anywhere?"

A vague recollection of breakfast and boiling water surfaced in Danielle's brain, but the sight of her dowry spread out in front of her was all that mattered.

She ran to the chest and yanked out the silver satin slippers, holding them protectively to her chest. "These are my mother's!"

"Yes, and she's dead," Marguerite said coldly.

The firm sound of hand meeting cheek rang out as Danielle gave her stepsister the hardest slap she could muster. To her satisfaction, the force of the blow sent Marguerite stumbling to the floor.

But Danielle wasn't finished yet.

"I am going to rip your hair out!" Danielle cried, chasing Marguerite around the bed and out of the room.

Fire burned inside her as she flew down the hallway after her stepsister. How dared Marguerite, with her greasy hands, touch anything that had belonged to Danielle's mother?

Gasping for breath, Danielle followed Marguerite into the drawing room. For several minutes they played a game of cat and mouse, Marguerite dodging behind furniture, Danielle shoving it aside, Marguerite sidestepping left and right, frantically trying to escape Danielle's furious grasp.

At last Danielle had Marguerite where she wanted her—in front of the fireplace. There was nowhere to run, nowhere to hide.

Danielle stepped forward, as Marguerite, desperate, dashed to the mantel and snatched up Danielle's beloved *Utopia.*

"Get away from me, or so help me, God . . . !" Marguerite warned, her cheeks flaming. She waved the novel perilously close to the fire.

"Put it down!" Danielle commanded, halting in midstep.

"Give me the shoes!" Marguerite demanded.

"Put it down!" Danielle yelled, hating her stepsister more than she had ever thought possible.

She was so focused on Marguerite that she barely noticed Rodmilla's entrance. "Consider carefully, Danielle," Rodmilla advised in her loftiest tone. "Your father's book or your mother's shoes . . . although neither will save you from a sound lashing."

The shoes are priceless to me, but Utopia *. . . I couldn't sleep at night without reading at least a* *few lines.* Wordlessly Danielle handed the slippers to Rodmilla, her eyes never leaving the book. She reached out to retrieve her father's last gift to her.

With a sickening smile, Marguerite dropped the book into the flames.

"No!" Danielle cried, running forward. Rodmilla grabbed and held her back.

Danielle watched, tears streaming down her cheeks, as her father's beloved treasure turned to ashes.

And the lump of despair that had formed in her stomach balled up into a cold, hard fist of anger.

Rodmilla took slow, mincing steps, twirling her parasol back and forth. It was important to walk not in front of the queen, but rather a step behind. She trusted Marguerite would remember. To be asked to walk in the royal gardens—and with the queen herself—was quite a coup.

Queen Marie's face was distressed as she reached over and patted Marguerite's hand. "To think that you saved that baby from a runaway horse. You really must have my doctor look at that." She gestured to the dark bruise that graced Marguerite's left eye.

Telling the queen that Marguerite's injury had

been caused by her doing a good deed had been a stroke of brilliance, if Rodmilla did say so herself.

"It was a maternal instinct, Majesty," Marguerite said demurely, running her finger over the lace trim of her dress.

"She is being modest," Rodmilla confided to the queen. She looked at Marguerite with admiration. Marguerite put on a humble expression. "Truth be told, she never does a thing for herself, always looking out for the less fortunate."

The queen smiled. "I am so sorry my son cannot join us. He seems to have disappeared again."

"Again?" Rodmilla repeated.

"Yes. He was gone all day yesterday and did not return until dawn." The queen shook her head in wonder.

Rodmilla thought of someone else who had been gone all day yesterday, someone who hadn't returned until dawn. Could it be? *No. That is utterly ridiculous.* "It would be marvelous to have that kind of stamina," she said instead.

"Perhaps you can help solve this mystery for me," the queen said as they turned down a row of exquisitely trimmed shrubbery. "Do you know the Comtesse de Lancret? Apparently she is visiting a cousin, but no one seems to know who."

Rodmilla nearly fainted into the hedgerow.

Lancret was the last name of Auguste's first wife—Danielle's mother! "*Nicole* de Lancret?" she asked, willing herself to remain calm.

"Yes!" The queen clapped her hands gleefully. "Oh, wonderful! I was beginning to think she was a ghost."

"No," Rodmilla replied, choosing her words carefully. "I am afraid she has been around for years . . . and . . . staying with us, as a matter of fact. Right, darling?"

Queen Marie seated herself on a marble bench, and Rodmilla and Marguerite followed suit.

Rodmilla smiled at her daughter, raising her eyebrows.

"Yes," Marguerite said under her mother's silent prompting, not understanding. "Of course. Our cousin."

"Whom you like to call Cinderella," Rodmilla said through gritted teeth.

Marguerite bolted up off the bench, her face red, her breath coming in short, ragged gasps.

For heaven's sake, sit down! Rodmilla thought exasperatedly. *Don't ruin it all now.*

Miraculously her daughter seemed to come to her senses. She sat abruptly, her manner composed.

"Good heavens, child, are you all right?" the

queen asked, waving a fan in front of Marguerite's crimson face.

The girl blinked. "There was a bee," she said faintly, nodding at a big pot of tulips on her left.

Rodmilla smiled apologetically at the queen and reached to take her daughter's arm.

Marguerite's reaction was understandable. But there was no need to fear.

Nicole de Lancret—or whoever Danielle thought she was—would never get away with this.

Danielle winced as Jacqueline applied ointment to her injured back. The two had been left alone in the house while Rodmilla and Marguerite attended some function at Hautefort. To Danielle's amazement, Jacqueline had knocked on her bedchamber door and asked if she could help. The lashing Rodmilla had given Danielle that afternoon had been brutal, perhaps the worst ever. Of course she couldn't see them, but Danielle knew the welts were severe.

"You really brought this on yourself, you know," Jacqueline said quietly, gently patting Danielle's throbbing skin with the ointment. "First with breakfast and then that horrid display downstairs."

"I wish yesterday had never happened,"

Danielle whispered, fighting back tears. The lashing was nothing new . . . but having Jacqueline comfort her was. Perhaps this stepsister wasn't as horrible as she'd thought.

Jacqueline snorted. "Of course, I shall never forget the way Marguerite's feet went up over her head like that. . . ." She chuckled and began wrapping soft bandages around Danielle's torso, clucking under her breath. "She should not have spoken so about your mother."

Danielle could not have agreed more.

After her back had been bandaged, Danielle thanked Jacqueline profusely, then got dressed as quickly as she could, tucking her hair into a white crocheted cap and applying a bit of borrowed rouge. She'd managed to borrow another dress from Gustave's studio—a beautiful red velvet with gathered white sleeves and a simple neckline. When the coast was clear, she tiptoed out of the house, hid her regular clothes behind a gnarled oak tree, and made her way to Amboise to meet the waiting prince.

The ruined cathedral was one of her favorite places to seek refuge. It lay deep in the forest, tucked away like a hidden jewel. Once, its towers had appeared to touch the sky, and majestic panels of stained glass had told the stories of the Bible, casting beams of colored light on the smooth stone floor. Now the ravaged cathedral was home to squirrels and chirping bluebirds instead of priests and nuns, its mossy floors standing fast, a reminder of what once had been.

Danielle walked silently through the grass. The trees cast deep shadows across the woodland. There, sitting on a window ledge, was Henry. He looked as beautiful as she'd ever seen him, his hair falling across his brow, his expression intense as he read from a leatherbound book. She felt guilty about disturbing him.

He looked up before she could speak, his lips curving into a welcoming smile.

"Hello," she said.

The prince hopped lightly to the ground. A tiny clutch of fear grabbed her stomach at the thought that he might touch her, and she instinctively stiffened. She was afraid that the slightest pressure of his hands on her back would make her faint.

"Are you well, *madame*?" His face was full of concern.

"I fear I am not myself today," Danielle replied, unable to miss the obvious happiness radiating from the prince's face.

His dark eyes glittered in the sunlight. "And I feel as if my skin is the only thing keeping me from going everywhere at once."

Danielle swallowed. She had come here to tell the prince the truth. She would have no misgivings. "There . . . there is something I must tell you."

"And I, you." He grinned.

"Your Highness—" Danielle began.

He smiled gently at her. "Henry."

"I cannot stay long, but I had to see you again," she said in a rush. "There is much to say."

"I have not slept for fear I would wake to find this all a dream. Last night I had a revelation," he told her, excitement filling his voice. "I used to think that if I cared about anything, I would have to care about everything, and that I would go stark raving mad." He took her hands. "But now I've found my purpose—a project, actually, inspired by you. And I feel the most wonderful freedom!"

Danielle's heart sank as Henry stared into her eyes. *He is truly the most wonderful man alive, and I am going to break his heart.* . . . "Henry, please, it wasn't me," she blurted out. "It's always been inside you. Never forget that. Promise me you won't forget that."

Henry looked at her adoringly. "You are unlike any courtier I have ever met, Nicole, and tomorrow at the masque I shall make that known to the world."

"Why did you have to be so wonderful?" Danielle whispered, choking back the lump that had formed in her throat.

"Now, then." Henry squeezed her hands. "What was it you wanted to tell me?"

"Simply that . . ." The unspoken words hung in the air . . . and Danielle let them vanish.

She couldn't do it.

". . . last night was the happiest night of my life," she said. Impulsively she threw her arms around him and kissed him with all her heart, all her soul. His lips warmed to hers, and for a few seconds nothing else mattered.

When Henry wrapped his arms tightly around Danielle, he unwittingly touched the welts under her bandages, and a shooting pain made its way up her spine . . . and straight into her heart.

"No!" she cried, breaking away.

Henry's eyes were filled with confusion. "I'm sorry."

Danielle stumbled backward, drinking in every last feature of his being . . . his compassionate eyes, his strong arms, his soft lips, his chiseled cheekbones, his sensitive soul . . .

"I must go," she murmured, a tear trickling down her cheek.

"Nicole—" Henry began.

She moved farther off, brushing him away

with her hand. "No, no, no . . ." Lifting the hem of her dress, she turned and fled through the forest.

By the time she returned to the manor, Danielle felt drained. She had cried a thousand tears as she ran blindly along the forest paths, unable to erase from her mind the stricken look on Henry's face as she had turned to leave. Slowly she undressed behind the old oak, carefully folding the red gown. She walked stiffly into the house, her legs carrying her rigid body forward, the consciousness of what she had lost weighing heavily on her shoulders.

Rodmilla and her daughters were waiting for her in the living room. *Just what I don't need.*

"Of all the insidious jokes, turning your mother into a comtesse," Rodmilla fumed, rising from the couch. "Why, it's almost as absurd as a prince spending his days with a servant who sleeps with pigs!"

Paulette, Louise, and Maurice cowered in the corner.

Danielle stared unflinchingly at Rodmilla, almost relieved that her ruse was out. "Which bothers you more, Stepmother? That I'm common? Or that I'm competition?"

Rodmilla glared at her. "Where is the dress?" she snapped.

Danielle shrugged. "I do not know what you are talking about."

"The gown, the slippers!" Marguerite exclaimed. "They were in my room this morning, and now they are gone! You hid them, I know it!"

"Where did you put the gown, Danielle?" Rodmilla asked, her voice tight.

"Where did you put the candlesticks?" Danielle countered. "Where are the tapestries? The silver? The mirrors? Perhaps the dress is with them." The thievery at the Manoir de Barbarac had not gone unnoticed by Danielle. She knew none of the staff could be responsible. Marguerite was too stupid, and Jacqueline was not that malicious. That left only one person.

Rodmilla reddened. "You will produce that gown *immediately,* or—"

"I will die a thousand deaths before I see my mother's dress on that spoiled, selfish cow!" Danielle shouted.

Marguerite gasped. Jacqueline coughed back a laugh. Rodmilla's eyes narrowed. "Well, perhaps we can arrange that," she said, grabbing Danielle's arm.

Danielle said nothing as Rodmilla yanked her down the hallway and motioned for her to step into the cold stone cellar. She said nothing as Rodmilla smiled cruelly and slammed the cellar door, plunging her into a world of darkness, a hole populated by rats and smelling of damp firewood. And she said nothing as Rodmilla's piercing voice echoed down the stairway.

"Open this door and you will wish you had never set foot in this house," her stepmother barked to the household. "Marguerite, Jacqueline, gather everything that will fetch a price. We are going to town first thing in the morning."

There was nothing Danielle could say. Nothing and no one would free her from this prison.

And nothing and no one could ever carry her into Henry's loving arms again.

Chapter Eight

"*T*he Comtesse Nicole de Lancret is already engaged?" Henry repeated weakly. "To a Belgian?" He sat down on the castle steps in disbelief.

"I am afraid so," Queen Marie said, patting his shoulder.

Henry shook his head. "That's impossible," he said defiantly. "There has to be some mistake." Beautiful, sweet, giving Nicole. There was no way she would have betrayed him like this. Was there?

The queen's voice was sympathetic. "She was traveling by boat this afternoon. The baroness was quite reluctant to talk about it."

"It is no wonder, with tidings such as these!" Henry exclaimed, his head in his hands. "If she was betrothed, she damn well should have had the decency to say something!"

"Would you have listened?" his mother asked gently.

"Of course not! I would have—" The image of Nicole came flooding back to him. She had been radiant in that red gown at Amboise as she backed away from him, a tear rolling down her cheek. Henry moaned. Suddenly it all made perfect, horrible sense.

"Oh, how could I have been so blind? There I was pouring my royal heart out and she was simply trying to bid me farewell."

The queen ruffled her son's hair. "It is a strong woman who keeps her wits about her with you trying to steal her heart."

"Yes, and what a clumsy thief I turned out to be," he said wretchedly, hating how pathetic he must have looked to Nicole.

"Come now, Henry, there are other choices," she said, trying to cheer him up.

Other choices? No, no other choices existed for him. Not in France, not in Europe, not in the entire universe. Henry had finally found the one woman he was meant to be with.

And she had pledged her love to someone else.

* * *

"It warms my heart to see a mother so devoted to her daughters." Pierre le Pieu dropped a handful of gold coins into Rodmilla's outstretched hand.

She sniffed. "It is a small sacrifice—"

"For such a large reward," he finished. He gestured at the elegantly furnished room around him. "But I fear, Baroness, your manor is empty. For as you can see, I am living in most of it."

Rodmilla didn't bother noting the mirrors, the paintings, and the candlesticks in le Pieu's display. She was well aware of every item she had had to sell off to this detestable man.

"After tonight, that manor can burn for all I care," she declared. That night the prince would choose Marguerite, her daughter would become a princess, and *she* would be living the life that rightfully belonged to her.

Le Pieu smiled crookedly. "And what of your Danielle?" he asked, hovering over her.

"What about her?" Rodmilla asked warily, repulsed by his stinking breath.

"I have always had a soft spot for the less fortunate, and even though I am old, I am well endowed." Rodmilla's ears perked up. "Unless, of course, you yourself have grown tired of your solitude." He wagged his scraggly eyebrows at her.

"Surely you jest," Rodmilla replied, taken aback.

"We are two sides of the same coin, Baroness. Our lives have been a constant struggle for respect. I plan to savor my revenge like a sumptuous meal." He licked his thin lips. "Perhaps we could dine together."

"I seem to have lost my appetite, *monsieur.* Good day." She pivoted quickly on her heel and headed for the door.

Le Pieu must really think her desperate to attempt to make a woman like her such an offer. Rodmilla smiled grimly. *After the ball, I will be in a position to tell him where to go. And it definitely will not be to my bedroom.*

The mere idea of it was sickening.

Gustave had told Maurice a thousand times that it was impossible. But the man would not listen to reason. "You are her friend, Gustave, she needs your help!" Maurice cried as the two men stood in the middle of the sunny village square. "He expects to see her!"

A wagon full of wine barrels rolled by them, sending a cloud of dust over Gustave's clothes. "But I am nobody!" Gustave protested, pointing to his threadbare shirt. "The prince would never see me."

Maurice would not hear this. "Then go to da Vinci! Surely a painter can see another painter. Find him!"

Gustave wanted to help Danielle, but how could he? And to speak to Signore da Vinci? "I am but an apprentice, sire, and he is the greatest painter in the world. I could no sooner talk to God."

He and Maurice watched as Rodmilla, Marguerite, and Jacqueline came out of a dressmaker's shop.

Maurice grabbed him by the shoulders and shook him hard. "For once in your life, man, be bold!"

Whether it was out of duty, love, or just plain insanity, Gustave didn't know, but at eight o'clock that evening, he found himself tumbling out from underneath a carriage and standing in front of the drawbridge of Hautefort.

The castle was ablaze with lights, and fireworks exploded over the towers as the masked ball officially began. Gustave watched as carriage after carriage discharged its costumed passengers. He spotted Rodmilla accompanied by two ladies, one in a feathery peacock mask, the other inside a clunky horse's head. He was so nervous that he couldn't even laugh.

He had to plan his move. He had to get into the castle. But how? At first he'd thought he'd simply stroll across the drawbridge, but members of the royal guard stood sentry at the front door, collecting invitations. He'd never be able to slip by them.

Out of the corner of his eye, he noticed the royal page sneaking off into a quiet corner. Just behind him on the wall sat a ceramic vase of flowers.

Gustave tiptoed up behind him.

"Wha—" the page gasped as he fastened his pants.

"Didn't anyone teach you to use the little boys' room?" Gustave asked, the vase in his hands. Then he smashed the page squarely on the head with it.

Dragging him farther into the darkness, Gustave undressed him and donned his uniform. A little tight, but it would do.

Now it was time for the rest of his mission.

Gustave moved stealthily through the well-heeled crowd, asking various partygoers if any of them had seen Signore da Vinci.

"Yes, he's over there," said a man dressed as a court jester. Or maybe he *was* the court jester. Gustave didn't know. *But a few laughs right now wouldn't hurt,* he thought nervously as he made his way toward the distinguished-looking gentleman with the long white beard.

Gustave's hands were moist with sweat as he drew near da Vinci. His throat was parched. His knees were shaking.

They would have been shaking even more if he had known he'd picked the wrong man . . . and that the real Leonardo da Vinci stood only a foot behind him.

"Si-Si-Signore da Vinci?" Gustave croaked.

And then he fainted . . . into the *real* Signore da Vinci's surprised arms.

"Oh, mistress, it's no use!" Paulette's muffled voice wailed.

Danielle bit her lip as she sat huddled on the damp wooden step. Despite Rodmilla's threat, her friends had been trying to pick the cellar lock for hours. *It is no use,* she thought dully. *Marguerite is sinking her claws into Henry this very minute.*

"Allow me."

The calm male voice startled Danielle. She stood. The sound of metal scraping metal filled the air, and in a matter of seconds the door was off its hinges.

"Brilliant!" Paulette cheered.

"Why, that was pure genius," Louise marveled.

"Yes, I shall go down in history as the man

who opened a door," said the man who was *holding* the door. He leaned the heavy wooden rectangle against the wall.

The sudden light stung her eyes, and Danielle blinked as her vision slowly came into focus. She stepped out of the cellar, her jaw dropping at the sight of her rescuers: her dear friend Gustave, standing alongside Signore da Vinci! "Gustave, how . . . ?"

He smiled. "Maurice said the prince was expecting you."

Danielle glanced at her mud-encrusted feet. "He's expecting someone who does not exist. *Signore,* my name is Danielle de Barbarac. I am but a servant."

Signore da Vinci moved beside her. "And I am the bastard son of a mason. What has that to do with anything?"

Danielle choked back tears of shame. "But I have deceived him!"

"My dear, the prince will understand," the artist assured her. "All anyone possesses in this life is his character, and yours is as noble as they come."

Paulette took her by the hand. "Come, child, the night is still young. We must get you ready for the ball."

"I do not wish to go," Danielle said, her eyes downcast.

"If you stay, the baroness wins and we all might as well join you down there in the pit," Louise said softly.

Danielle looked around her. The people she held most dear in the world: Paulette, Louise, Maurice. Each of them looking at her with hope, each of them wanting the best for her, as they always had. *But what if I disappoint them? What if—*

She turned to Signore da Vinci. "How can I face him?" she implored.

"Because he deserves to hear the truth from the one he loves," he answered.

She managed a tiny smile. "A bird may love a fish, *Signore,* but where would they live?"

The artist pulled her into his arms and wrapped them tenderly around her. "Then I shall have to make you wings."

Danielle took a seat at the large kitchen table as Signore da Vinci rummaged through his leather satchel, pulling out paintbrushes, powders, and little tubes of paint. Paulette, Louise, and Maurice gathered around her excitedly.

The artist laid out his supplies on the table. He cupped Danielle's tear-stained face in his hands, took a clean cloth from Paulette, and dipped it into the pail of water that sat in the corner. He gently wiped Danielle's cheeks.

And then he began to paint.

The feathery strokes of the brush tickled her face. She had to force herself to keep still. "I don't understand," she said as da Vinci dipped his paintbrush into some white powder. "If I'm to arrive as myself, is it not wrong to perform such magic on me?"

Signore da Vinci smiled at her. "I suppose it would be if it weren't already a masked ball. Rest assured, Danielle, there is no alchemy here; no deceit." He began to apply tiny feathers along her hairline. "God gives each of us our own gifts, but it is up to us to apply them, to nurture them, and to trust them."

Her friends nodded, entranced by the transformation the artist was effecting.

Da Vinci smoothed back her hair. "A seed planted in the parched earth doesn't stand a chance. But with a few sunny days, some water . . . some love . . . anything is possible. To blossom is to live, Danielle. *You* are the only magic here."

A solitary tear fell down her cheek, and Danielle blinked, not wanting to destroy what Signore da Vinci was taking such pains to create.

Perhaps the mask would give her strength, she reasoned. She could be someone else for a little while that night . . . a magical fairy princess, a grown-up version of the little girl she once had been.

A fairy princess who needed to tell her fairy-tale prince the truth.

Night had fallen on the castle grounds, and Rodmilla and her daughters had decided to make a promenade through the gardens before the masque officially began. "This way you'll have a basic knowledge of the gardens," she had told a tittering Marguerite. "You'll need to be informed about this sort of thing when you become the princess."

Rodmilla adjusted her mask, which was sticking lightly to her face. The night air was warm, and Rodmilla had just decided to head back into the castle when Pierre le Pieu strolled past them, a fancily dressed woman on each arm.

Rodmilla straightened her back as the trio walked past.

"Good evening, ladies," le Pieu said with a nod.

Rodmilla frowned at him. "It was until you showed up."

Le Pieu gave Marguerite the once-over. "I

daresay, Marguerite, that the man who wins your affections will be the luckiest man in the kingdom."

"Yes, and the women who delight in your company, *monsieur*, aren't paid nearly enough," Marguerite replied tartly.

Rodmilla stifled a laugh. The two women with le Pieu were what was delicately referred to as "ladies of the night."

"You do have an agile tongue," le Pieu said.

Before her daughter could engage in any more banter with this disreputable character, Rodmilla hustled her and Jacqueline into the castle ballroom.

The masque was about to begin.

They only had to elbow four women and crush the toes of five others to secure the first spots in the receiving line. Their positions were excellent . . . and guaranteed that they would be in full view of the prince as he made his grand entrance.

Rodmilla pinched Marguerite's arm as Prince Henry entered the ballroom. He looked absolutely dashing in his jewel-toned tunic and black breeches. *He and Marguerite will have the most divine babies,* she thought dreamily. As the prince came to a stop in front of them, she curtsied. "Your Highness."

He smiled. "Baroness, Marguerite."

"A splendid evening, sire," Rodmilla said, making sure to strike just the right note of admiration and respect.

"Yes, quite." He glanced past them. "Is it just the two of you?"

"Jacqueline is at the buffet," Rodmilla said confidentially. She'd made sure her youngest daughter was safely out of the way. *Not that Jacqueline would ever have had a chance with the prince!* She almost laughed aloud at the thought.

"Well, since I am one of the hosts, I should probably ask one of you to dance," Henry said politely.

Marguerite latched on to his arm like a pit bull. "Love to!"

Gustave let out a contented sigh as Danielle stepped into Signore da Vinci's carriage. The crystal beads on her silver satin slippers shimmered in the moonlight. He and the staff collected themselves outside the manor to watch her go.

"She looks like a masterpiece," Gustave said, awed.

Louise clutched Maurice's hand. "She looks like her mother."

As the carriage pulled away, Signore da Vinci

put his paint-spattered arm around Gustave's shoulder. "Come," he said. "Let us go see these paintings of yours."

"Now?" Gustave gulped nervously.

"When you are as old as I am, my young friend, 'now' is all you've got."

Gustave nodded, and the two new friends began walking back toward the manor.

"Wait!" Paulette called. "It's tradition."

Gustave and Signore da Vinci turned and, along with the servants, watched as the carriage reached the main gate of the Manoir de Barbarac.

Then a small hand popped out of the carriage window . . . and waved.

Back at Hautefort, the masque was in full swing. While the king searched in vain for his guest of honor, Signore da Vinci, his guests danced in a ballroom filled with flowers and flaming torches, their light casting a magical glow on the myriad masks and costumes. Hungry revelers found their way to the lavish buffet table, which groaned under the weight of immense assortments of cheeses, clusters of sweet grapes and plums, berries and tangerines, asparagus and mushrooms, platters of roasted suckling pig and tenderly braised beef, pitchers full of wine, and the most delicate-looking pastries France had ever seen.

Jacqueline was in heaven—except for the stupid horse mask her mother had talked her into wearing. Rodmilla had assured her she'd be the "prettiest filly at the ball," and like a fool, she'd believed her. *The sweatiest is more like it,* Jacqueline thought as she piled her plate with cheese and hunks of crusty bread. It wasn't exactly a mask—it was more of a horse helmet.

She was halfway through the buffet when she reached for a crudité . . . and found someone else reaching for the very vegetable she had chosen.

Another horse.

"Whoa," said the horse, removing his mask.

Jacqueline blushed. Her equine neighbor was none other than Captain Laurent.

She took off her mask as well, giving him a playful smile. "Neigh."

Henry stood silently in the shadows of the tunnel that ran under Hautefort. He wanted to speak with his father privately, away from the hordes of guests who roamed the castle grounds. After Henry had waited only a few minutes, his father, accompanied by an entourage of torch-bearing servants, came down the hallway.

"I understand you wanted to see me," his father said.

"Yes, Father, I did."

The king examined Henry's face and, with a wave of his hand, dismissed the servants. "Listen, Henry, perhaps it was unfair of me to put so much pressure on you like this," the king began. "I just thought that it was time to make some changes in your life. You seemed to be floundering . . . and, well, I just wanted to tell you I think this university thing is a brilliant idea. We don't have to announce anything tonight if—"

Henry cut him off. "I've made my decision."

His father was momentarily stunned. "Oh. Well, that's fine," he said after a few seconds. "Fine. So who's the lucky girl?"

Henry stared off into the dark recesses of the tunnel. What did it matter who she was?

She wasn't the one he wanted.

Celeste reached out to the baroness. "Rodmilla, I trust you won't forget us little people," she said in a fawning tone.

Rodmilla gave the courtier a supercilious smile. "Oh, Celeste, I think you should count on it." She squeezed Marguerite's perspiring palm. This was the moment they had been waiting for, planning for . . . and now it was all coming true, in front of the entire kingdom. She snapped to attention as King Francis took the royal dais, Prince Henry on his left, Queen Marie on his right.

King Francis cleared his throat. "Friends, honored guests, it gives us great pride on this festive occasion to announce the engagement of our son, Prince Henry the First, to—"

Rodmilla almost fell forward in anticipation. She watched as the prince clamped a hand on his father's shoulder, his expression stunned as he stared at the great staircase that formed the entrance to the ballroom. The king stopped his speech and followed the prince's gaze.

Rodmilla followed it too, afraid to find out what they were looking at.

There, at the top of the stairs, stood the most magnificently costumed woman she had ever seen. Her face was a blend of feathers, powder, and pearls, and her honey brown hair was swept up in glorious curls. Gossamer wings extended from the back of her filmy white gown, fluttering gently in the evening breeze from the doorway.

A gasp rose from the crowd.

The prince went pale.

But Rodmilla only gripped Marguerite's trembling fingers more tightly and said nothing. She was too busy choking on her own rage.

Chapter Nine

*D*anielle had not expected every eye in the kingdom to be on her. She had thought she'd slip in, have a bite to eat, dance a few minuets, reveal her story to the prince ...

"Breathe, just breathe," she told her quaking self.

Directly across the room stood Henry—gorgeous, intelligent Henry. For a moment he stood as if paralyzed. Then he leaped off the dais and bounded across the ballroom to the top of the staircase where she stood. Her heart was in her throat as he took her face in his soft hands and looked yearningly into her eyes.

"Tell me it is really you," he begged.

Danielle nodded nervously. The guests were hanging on their every word. "I have come disguised as myself."

Henry shook his head in amazement. "My mother said you were getting married."

"She was misinformed." Danielle steadied herself. "Henry, there is something I must tell you, now, before another word is spoken."

"Then you are not engaged?" he blurted out, gripping her hands.

The heat between them was almost unbearable. "No. I am not."

She swallowed as the gigantic tower bell began to strike the twelve peals of midnight.

One.

"I was about to make the worst mistake of my life," Henry said, his face glowing. "Come. There is someone I want you to meet."

She accepted his hand, and he led her down the staircase. *Please, don't let me trip in front of all these people.* Danielle lifted her gown to descend, unwittingly putting her beaded slippers into the spotlight, where they sparkled brilliantly, dazzling the crowd.

"Henry, I must speak with you!" Danielle said urgently as they reached the bottom of the stairs.

Two.

"Whatever it is, my answer is yes," Henry said, shushing her. "Oh, and look, look! I invited the Gypsies."

Three.

Danielle glanced their way and smiled, but her nerves were in such a state that she could barely breathe.

The crowd parted as the couple crossed the room to the royal dais. Suddenly Danielle felt a sharp tug on her wings. She tottered.

"How dare you!" Rodmilla shrieked, flying at her like a bat out of hell. She reached up and yanked at the gossamer wings.

Four.

Danielle shrank back in horror as Henry pushed Rodmilla away. "*Madame,* contain yourself!" he shouted, obviously appalled.

"She is an impostor, sire!" Rodmilla cried. A hush fell over the crowd.

"No!" Danielle burst out as her world shattered before her eyes.

Five.

"Her name is Danielle de Barbarac, and she has been a servant in my home for the past ten years," Rodmilla spat out, her eyes in narrow slits.

King Francis materialized beside them. "A servant, Henry? Is this some kind of joke?"

Henry's face had gone from crimson to snow white. "Baroness, you are on dangerous ground!" he warned.

Six.

"Ask her yourself!" Rodmilla shot back. "She's a grasping, devious little pretender." She stomped her foot. "And it is my duty, Your Highness, to expose this deception as the covetous hoax it is!"

Henry turned to Danielle, confused and embarrassed. "Tell these women who you are," he said, nodding encouragingly. "Tell them."

Seven.

Danielle looked at him, pain wrenching her heart. She grasped for the right words, but all that came out was a tiny whimper.

"Tell them," he practically begged, his voice unsteady.

Danielle was mute.

Eight.

"My God," Henry whispered, backing away. "It cannot be true."

Rodmilla pushed forward so that she was practically nose to nose with the cowering Danielle. "Bow before royalty, you insolent fraud!"

"Nicole . . ." Henry looked utterly destroyed.

Nine.

"Nicole de Lancret was my mother, Your

157

Highness," Danielle managed to say, the blood throbbing in her temples. "I am who this woman says."

The hushed crowd began to murmur excitedly, pressing in closer.

Henry blinked in disbelief, his eyes suddenly growing wide. "The apples? That was *you*?"

Ten.

"I can explain!" Danielle cried.

King Francis pounded his scepter on the ground. "Well, someone had better!"

Henry laughed coldly. "First you're engaged and now you're a servant. I've had enough." He turned to leave.

"Henry, please!" Danielle cried, throwing all caution to the wind. It wasn't the prince she loved, it was *Henry*. Henry who had laughed with her in the Gypsy cave, who had showed her books filled with wonderful stories and legends, who had guided her horse right to her doorstep, who had kissed her as if she were the most special person in the world . . .

The crowd gasped at her familiarity.

Eleven.

Henry spun around. "Do not address me so informally, *mademoiselle*. I am a prince of France, and you are . . . just . . . like . . . them."

His words were hurtful enough, but it was the

look on his face—the look of utter betrayal—that Danielle could not bear to see. She turned and fled through the flabbergasted crowd.

Twelve.

Leonardo da Vinci walked slowly up the magnificent royal driveway. The sight of the castle illuminated at night always stunned him, and that night, with the torches blazing brightly along the drawbridge and the remnants of fireworks scenting the air, it was positively breathtaking.

A flash of white attracted his attention, and he watched as a young woman came running from the castle and across the drawbridge. She looked desperate to get away, and in her haste she tripped and fell just as she reached the outside gate.

A tiny slipper fell off her foot.

Leonardo caught his breath. "Danielle!" he cried.

But she didn't stop, only raced onward.

The artist hurried forward and picked up the abandoned shoe, still warm from her foot. What could have happened to make her flee like this?

A low rumble of thunder sounded in the distance. As the first drops of rain began to fall, a worried Leonardo made his way into the ballroom and out onto the castle balcony.

Only one person knew the reason for Danielle's misery.

And that person was standing in the rain, water trickling down his face. "My God, Henry, what have you done?" Leonardo asked, walking to him.

The prince was stone-faced. "I have been born to privilege, and with that come specific obligations."

Leonardo was outraged at the young man's attitude. "Horse manure."

Prince Henry's lips drew together. "You are out of line, old man."

"No, *you* are out of line," Leonardo said angrily. "Do you have any idea what that girl went through to get here tonight?"

"She lied to me!"

Leonardo put his hands on his head in frustration. "She came to tell you the truth and you fed her to the wolves!"

"What do you know?" Henry scoffed, running his fingers through his wet hair. He waved his arm in the air. "You build flying machines and walk on water, and yet you know nothing about life!"

"I know that a life without love is no life at all," the artist told the young man quietly.

"And love without trust? What of that?" the prince demanded testily.

"She is your match, Henry!" Leonardo declared.

The prince stared out into the vast sea of blackness that surrounded the castle. His eyes were void of emotion. "I am but a servant to my crown, and I have made my decision. I will not yield."

Leonardo's heart filled with pity as he thought of the beautiful Danielle, worthy of any man's praise. "You don't deserve her," he said. He reached under his cloak and withdrew Danielle's slipper. Placing it on the balcony ledge, he walked slowly back into the castle, leaving the prince standing alone in the rain.

Danielle's return home had been quite a different experience from her departure. No friends were there to greet her as she limped barefoot up the muddy drive. No artist was there to turn her smeared face into a fairy masterpiece.

After burning her wind-shredded wings, gown, and remaining slipper in a small fire, she'd spent the night curled up on the sodden barn floor, listening to the pounding of the rain on the roof, sleeping barely an hour. She'd risen early and headed straight for the field behind the manor, where she picked up a hoe and attacked the moistened dirt with a vengeance.

"Danielle?" came a voice from the terrace.

It was Rodmilla.

"I have it on good authority that before your rather embarrassing debut, the prince was about to choose Marguerite for his bride," she announced, folding her arms.

Danielle ignored her. Dropping the garden tool, she scooped up a basket of freshly picked vegetables and headed up the walk.

"Men are so fickle," Rodmilla said, chuckling. "One minute they're spouting sonnets, and the next you're back to being the hired help."

I will not give her the satisfaction, Danielle thought bitterly. *Nothing she can say or do can hurt me now . . . I'm way beyond hurt.*

"But I must say, I've never seen you quite this dedicated to your chores," Rodmilla observed drolly.

Danielle continued walking. "What makes you think I do any of this for you?" she asked.

"Well, aren't we feisty this morning?"

As Danielle reached the manor's back door, Rodmilla blocked her path, a smug look on her face.

"Let me pass," Danielle said.

"You brought this on yourself, you know."

Danielle looked at her stepmother with cold,

hard eyes. "Don't you understand? *You've won!* Go! Move into the palace and leave us be!"

"You are not my problem anymore," Rodmilla said cryptically.

Danielle turned on her heel and headed for the front of the manor, trying to remain calm. Like a trained dog, Rodmilla was right at her heels. "Your problem?" Danielle said, stung. "I have done everything you asked, and still you denied me the only thing I ever wanted!"

"And what was that?" Rodmilla asked.

Danielle shook her head, amazed at her stepmother's question. "What do you think?"

Just then Paulette poked her head out of an upstairs window. "Mistress! Danielle! Come see! It's back, all of it!" she called.

But Danielle was not to be stopped. "You are the only mother I have ever known," she told Rodmilla. "Was there ever a time, even in its smallest measurement, that you loved me at all?"

Rodmilla stared back at her, incredulous. "How can anyone love a pebble in their shoe?"

An incredible wave of sadness came over Danielle. After years of mistreatment, she had known that Rodmilla did not love her like a daughter. But deep down, a tiny part of her had always hoped, always believed, that this woman who had married her father must have some feelings of love and kindness for her.

That hope was gone.

"Frankly, I've never understood why you've stayed on as long as you have," Rodmilla continued.

Danielle faced her. "Because one day you will be dead and this manor will still be here . . . and so will I," she said, pride burning inside her. "You have been a trespasser in my father's house far too long."

Danielle rounded the corner of the house. A caravan of carts loaded with furniture and household goods was parked outside. Pierre le Pieu stood in front of them.

"Ah, Monsieur le Pieu," Rodmilla greeted him warmly. "Right on time."

"It's all here, Baroness. Every last candlestick."

Danielle gazed at the carts' contents. There was the painting that had hung for years in the manor's hallway . . . the carved writing desk her father had used to compose letters . . . the silver platter Paulette had served last year's Christmas dinner on.

Slowly it all began to fall into place.

"The paintings . . . my father's books . . . you sold them to *him*?" Danielle asked, her voice cracking.

"Yes, and now they're back," Rodmilla replied.

"I couldn't very well have us looking like paupers when the king arrives."

Danielle stared at the debauched court armorer in wonder. "*Monsieur,* thank you!" she cried, overcome. "This means the world to us."

Le Pieu shrugged. "I am a businessman, Danielle, not a philanthropist."

Danielle looked from him to Rodmilla. "I don't understand."

Her stepmother sighed. "I can't very well have you around distracting the prince, now, can I?" She and le Pieu exchanged knowing glances.

"The baroness and I have an agreement," le Pieu began.

"You, for all this," Rodmilla finished. "Although I do think I'm getting the better end of the deal."

Raw horror hit Danielle like a slap in the face. Her stepmother had sold her to that slimy le Pieu! Before she had time to gather her wits, le Pieu's henchmen jumped down from the carts and grabbed her roughly by the arms.

"No! Let me go!" she cried, kicking and screaming. Maurice tried vainly to stop the men but was shoved aside.

Tears streamed down her face as she was tossed inside le Pieu's cramped carriage and heard the door being shut and bolted.

She was a prisoner.

I wish I were dead, she thought as the carriage bumped down the road, taking her away from the only home she'd ever had.

Trumpets blasted. Horns blared. Bushels of fragrant roses and fleur-de-lis had been carted in, windows had been washed, floors scrubbed, the woodcarvings polished. The cardinal had been summoned from Paris.

After all, it wasn't as if a royal wedding happened every day.

Light filtered down on Prince Henry, dressed in full uniform, as he stood rigidly at the cathedral's ornate altar. Behind him choirboys sang hymns in Latin as France's finest musicians accompanied them. King Francis and Queen Marie were seated in the front pew, surrounded by the members of the royal court.

Jacqueline dabbed her eyes. The congregation stood for the bride as she passed down the aisle. The bride was a vision in white silk and lace, a mantilla covering her face, head, and shoulders. Weddings always made Jacqueline cry.

Reaching the altar, the bride stood by the prince's side. The music stopped. And then Jacqueline could hear it—*everyone* could hear it—the bride was *crying*. Loudly. The church was silent but for the sound of the bride's weeping. As she stood by her intended, her shoulders were racked with sobs.

Jacqueline glanced at her mother ... and Marguerite, who stood glumly by her side, each lost in a fantasy of what might have been. Then Jacqueline looked once more at the bride, who, as the cardinal began the ceremony, turned and looked back at a short, bald man crying softly in the third row. *Who could he be?* Jacqueline wondered.

The bride and groom knelt at the altar.

The cardinal began saying the wedding mass in Latin. Every word brought a new sniffle from the bride.

Jacqueline noticed that the more tears the bride shed, the more the prince looked as if he was going to burst into laughter. To everyone's surprise, the prince motioned for the cardinal to stop, and he helped the shaking bride to her feet. Gently he lifted her veil, revealing a babbling, teary-eyed Princess Gabriella of Spain.

The prince gave her a big kiss on the cheek. "*Señorita*, I know exactly how you feel!" Nodding his approval, he smiled as his bride rushed from the altar and into the arms of the bald man.

Jacqueline couldn't believe it. Here, in front of all these people, the prince had put true love first. Smiling at the wonder of it all, she glanced across the pews and came eye-to-eye with Captain Laurent. He looked absolutely dashing that day . . . even more so when he noticed Jacqueline and flashed her a brilliant smile. He began to make his way to the back of the cathedral.

I think this would be just the right time to excuse myself, Jacqueline thought excitedly.

"Where is she?" Henry gasped, bursting out of the cathedral and spotting Rodmilla's servant Maurice next to her carriage. Being jilted at the altar was far from a tragedy . . . it was a blessing.

"The baroness?" Maurice asked, bowing to the prince.

Henry shook his head impatiently. "Danielle."

Maurice's face was filled with sorrow. "She has been sold, sire."

"Sold!" Henry exclaimed. "To whom?"

"Pierre le Pieu, Your Highness."

Rodmilla's daughter Jacqueline hurried over to them, her arm linked with Captain Laurent's. "It happened just after the masque," she told him ruefully.

Henry's blood churned inside his veins as he

remembered the way he had treated Danielle at the masque. Nicole, Comtesse, Danielle . . . none of it mattered. Signore da Vinci had been right. Danielle was an incredible woman, and he had been a fool to let her go.

He only hoped it wasn't too late to get her back.

Chapter Ten

"Enter," le Pieu called from his library inside the Château Beynac.

Danielle shuffled into the musty room, her face dripping with sweat. The revolting old man had clamped iron cuffs around her wrists and ankles, and the heavy metal felt like fire on a sweltering day like this one. She handed him the swords he had asked her to fetch.

"I do hate to see you in irons," he reflected. "I would remove them if you'd promise not to run away again."

"I have no reason to stay," Danielle said curtly. No matter how many times he stopped her, she would escape from this prison.

Le Pieu leered at her. "You belong to me now."

"I belong to no one," Danielle corrected him. "Least of all you."

He got up from his desk and lifted the sweaty clumps of hair off her back. "I do wish you would reconsider my offer."

Danielle recoiled. "I would rather rot."

"I had a horse like you once," le Pieu said thoughtfully. "Magnificent creature. Stubborn, like you, willful. It too just needed to be broken."

Danielle shuddered at the analogy. "You will maintain your distance, sir."

"You didn't say please," he said flirtatiously, slipping his oily arms around her.

Quickly Danielle turned to face him, placing the tip of a dagger she'd hidden behind her skirts to his chin. "Please."

"I could hang you for this," le Pieu growled, one eye on her, one eye on the point of the dagger.

"Not if you are dead," Danielle replied.

"I do love your spirit," le Pieu said, slamming her slender wrist down hard on the desk. Despite her shackled feet, Danielle was able to move aside, drawing the dagger along his face.

Le Pieu stumbled back, his hand touching his cheek. A trickle of blood oozed from the wound. Enraged, he grabbed one of the swords she had brought to him.

"My father was an expert swordsman, *monsieur*," Danielle told him, grabbing the other sword in her free hand and circling him. "He taught me well." She stared pointedly at the ring of keys that dangled from le Pieu's pocket. "Now, hand me that key, or I swear on his grave, I will slit you from navel to nose."

She prepared herself to fight as le Pieu started to call her bluff. Her eyes blazed as he neared, her hands gripping the sword handles.

Slowly le Pieu took the key from his pocket.

She had won.

After the perverted old goat had freed her from her chains, she locked him in them instead, hiding the key in the outer hallway. By the time he found it she would be far, far away.

Danielle marched outside the Château Beynac—and came face-to-face with Henry and the royal guard.

"Hello," Henry said shyly.

"Hello," Danielle said, taken aback. "What are you doing here?"

"I, uh, came to . . . rescue you."

She began to walk down the wide stone steps. "Rescue me?" she repeated innocently. "A commoner?"

"Actually I came to beg your forgiveness,"

Henry went on in a rush. "I offered you the world, and at the first test of honor I betrayed your trust. Please, Danielle . . ."

Danielle stopped. "Say it again."

"I'm sorry." Henry hung his head.

She smiled. "No. I meant the part when you said my name."

A relieved smile broke out on his face. "Danielle . . . perhaps you would be so kind as to help me find the owner of this rather remarkable shoe." He reached into his coat pocket and pulled out the exquisite silver satin slipper.

"Where did you get that?" Danielle gasped.

Henry stared at her with deep, intense eyes. "She is my match in every way. Please tell me I haven't lost her."

Danielle sank down on the step. "It belongs to a peasant, Your Highness, who only pretended to be a courtier to save a man's life."

"Yes, I know . . . and the name's Henry, if you don't mind," he said gently.

Her heart felt as if someone were squeezing it as he dropped to his knee. "I kneel before you not as a prince but as a man in love. But I would feel like a king if you, Danielle de Barbarac, would be my wife."

As if it were a dream, Danielle watched as he

slipped the shoe onto her foot. Of course it fit perfectly. She burst into tears and collapsed into his arms.

"Yes, yes, yes," she murmured happily into Henry's ear, kissing his hair, his neck, and then his tender lips. "Oh, yes."

Chapter Eleven

*J*acqueline took a nervous sip of consommé. Usually mealtime was one of the day's high points . . . but that night the tension in the dining room was so thick you could cut it with a knife.

Or you could fling your knife on the table, which was exactly what her mother did. "How could you be so stupid?" she ranted, looking daggers at Jacqueline.

Jacqueline cringed. "How was I to know he'd come flying out the side door?" she said, the soup roiling in her stomach. "He was supposed to be getting married!" When the prince had burst out of the cathedral, she'd been completely taken by surprise . . . but then she'd also been quite taken by Captain Laurent, who was becoming quite a special friend.

"People said he talked to you," Marguerite said. "What did he say?"

Jacqueline fidgeted with her napkin. "I can't be sure. . . . it all happened so quickly," she began. "But I think what he said was . . . 'Serves me right for choosing a foreigner over . . . your sister.'"

A self-satisfied smile appeared on her mother's face. "Well, then, perhaps we shall let him fret about it for a few days."

A bell sounded at the front door. "I'll get it!" the three women shouted in unison.

Rodmilla was the first to reach the door.

Captain Laurent (or Laurent, as Jacqueline had begun to call him in private) stood on the landing. He bowed. "His Supreme Majesty, King Francis, requests an audience with the Baroness Rodmilla de Ghent and her daughters immediately."

Jacqueline's heart palpitated at the sight of the dashing guardsman . . . and at the anticipation of the event she knew was about to take place.

Her mother licked her lips. "Is anything . . . wrong?"

Captain Laurent shook his head. "No, milady, the king demanded that you arrive in style."

Rodmilla took each of her daughters by the

arm and gave the captain a brilliant smile. "Then in style we shall be."

Never had so much speedy primping and powdering gone on in the Manoir de Barbarac as took place in preparation for the visit to Hautefort. But Rodmilla hadn't been caught completely unaware. *After all, I have been planning for this day for quite some time. A few trouble spots cropped up, to be sure, but they are all taken care of now.* And speaking of being taken care of, Rodmilla glowed with the knowledge that soon Marguerite would be married to the prince, and *she* would be taking up residence at Hautefort. *I've got to remind Marguerite that I want a room with a courtyard view.*

Rodmilla practically oozed with pride as she, Marguerite, and Jacqueline were welcomed into the great hall at Hautefort and were escorted to the throne room. Rodmilla had selected the most exquisite of dresses for herself and her daughters, making sure that Marguerite's was the finest. The effort had been well worthwhile, as every eye in the royal court was on them. They walked regally down the center aisle toward the royal dais, where King Francis and Queen Marie were seated on their thrones, the prince standing between them.

With great dignity, Rodmilla nodded to

Leonardo da Vinci and the members of the royal court, including Celeste and Isabelle. The satisfaction of this moment would thrill her for a long, long time.

The reception she got was a rude jolt. King Francis addressed her angrily. "Baroness, did you or did you not lie to Her Royal Majesty, the Queen of France?"

The queen's face was somber. "Choose your words wisely, *madame*, for they may be your last."

Rodmilla began to sweat. How had they found out? "A woman will do practically anything for the love of a daughter," she said desperately. She forced a laugh. "Perhaps I did get a little carried away."

Marguerite covered her mouth with her hand. "Mother, what have you done?" She turned an apologetic face to the queen. "Your Majesty, like you, I am just a victim here. She has lied to both of us, and I am ashamed to call her family!"

Rodmilla's fury was so great that she forgot where she was—and who was watching. "How *dare* you turn on me, you little ingrate?" she spat out, yanking her daughter by the arm so roughly that Marguerite's teeth chattered.

"You see?" Marguerite told the king self-righteously. "You see what I put up with?"

The king was not amused. "Silence! Both of

you!" He turned to Jacqueline. "Good lord, are they always like this?"

Jacqueline nodded solemnly. "Worse, Your Majesty."

"Jacqueline, darling," Rodmilla said, struggling to keep her voice light. "I'd hate to think *you* had anything to do with this."

Jacqueline smiled innocently. "Of course not, Mother. I'm only here for the food."

Queen Marie rose to her feet. "Baroness Rodmilla de Ghent, you are hereby stripped of your title, and you and your horrible daughter are to be shipped to the Americas on the next available boat, unless, by some miracle, someone here will speak for you."

A deadly silence fell over the royal court.

Rodmilla cast around hopefully for a friendly face. A decent face. A face that looked just the least bit helpful. But all she got were stony, unsympathetic glances. She turned back to the king. *I will not lose face over this! I still have my pride,* she thought, incensed by her treatment.

"There seem to be quite a few people out of town," she said, swallowing hard.

"I will speak for her," said a soft voice from the doorway.

Rodmilla spun around as the crowd gasped in astonishment. The sight that met her eyes was more horrible than any nightmare she'd ever had: Danielle in a beautiful gown, with a crown of rubies and diamonds glittering atop her head.

Rodmilla felt as if she would faint on the spot. Every particle of her being was shouting out *No!*, but it appeared that . . . that . . . Danielle was . . . was . . . a member of the court! Rodmilla's heart began to beat wildly, and she gasped like a fish out of water.

"She is, after all, my stepmother," Danielle added courteously.

Rodmilla watched, dumbstruck, as Danielle moved through the throne room. The entire court bowed as she passed.

Danielle curtsied before the king and queen. *She's on their good side!* Rodmilla thought with sudden alarm.

Danielle spoke. "All I would ask, Your Majesties, is that you show her the same courtesies she bestowed on me."

Henry stepped forward, a silly grin on his handsome face. "I don't believe you've met my wife," he said to Rodmilla and Marguerite.

Marguerite began to cry.

With all the self-control she could muster, Rodmilla slowly lowered herself to the floor. "Your . . . Highness," she choked.

Danielle's expression was restrained, but her eyes were lit with an intensity directed at Rodmilla. "I want you to know that I will forget you after this moment and never think of you again. But you, I am quite certain, will think of me every single day for the rest of your life."

"And how long might that be?" Rodmilla dared to ask, her fingers crossed.

Danielle locked eyes with her husband and smiled calmly back at Rodmilla. "I hope it's forever."

"And after you wash the tablecloths, you can start on the napkins." The portly washerwoman who supervised the palace laundry crew gestured to the mountain of dirty linens behind her.

Rodmilla's annoyance was reaching its limit. She stared down at herself, still unable to believe that not only had she been stripped of her title, but she'd also been stripped of her beautiful clothes—and given this horrible smock and disgusting work boots. Worse yet, she and Marguerite had been assigned laundry duty for an unspecified period. They'd spent the past three hours sorting dirty royal garments in the stuffy basement laundry room, and she'd had enough.

"And put these over there," the washerwoman

continued, tilting her head toward two bags of clothes that had just come down the chute.

"Marguerite," Rodmilla snapped.

"What?" Her daughter's face was red from exertion . . . a completely new experience for her.

"You heard the woman."

Marguerite gaped. "So did you."

"Yes, but I'm management," Rodmilla said, adjusting her frowzy kerchief.

Marguerite hooted. "The hell you are! Why, you're just the same as I am: a big nobody!"

"How dare you speak to me in such a tone!" Rodmilla shouted, throwing a rouge-stained napkin at her. "I am of noble blood, and you—"

"Are getting on my nerves!" barked the washerwoman. She picked up a heavy bag of laundry and flung it at Rodmilla and Marguerite, knocking the two into a giant vat of dirty water and making the other workers howl with laughter. "Now, get back to work!"

Danielle curled her arms around her husband as they galloped through the dusky night air toward the Manoir de Barbarac. The sun was just setting, casting a pinkish red glow on the shingled roof of her father's house. As she'd expected, all her friends—Paulette, Louise, and Maurice, along with the wonderful new staff Henry had hired—were waiting in front of the manor for them.

And inside was an even better surprise: the soon-to-be married Jacqueline and Captain Laurent, Gustave, and Signore da Vinci.

They gathered in the drawing room, in the middle of which stood an object covered with white muslin. With a flourish, the artist removed the cloth. Underneath was a breathtaking portrait of Danielle.

"Oh, Leonardo, it's wonderful!" Danielle exclaimed joyously.

Leonardo bowed. "Think of it as a belated wedding present, Your Highness."

Gustave snorted.

"What?" Danielle asked, looking at him.

"I still can't get over it. 'Your Highness.' "

Henry scratched his chin. "I must say, Leonardo, for a man of your talent, it doesn't look a thing like her."

Danielle gave him a playful jab. "You, sir, are supposed to be charming."

She sighed with happiness as Henry slipped his arms around her, kissing her softly on the lips. "And we, Princess, are supposed to live happily ever after."

"Says who?" Danielle teased.

A faraway look came to her husband's eyes. "You know, I don't know."

Danielle snuggled in close, breathing in Henry's clean, woodsy scent and pressing her cheek against his. Happily ever after . . . what a romantic way to begin the rest of their lives together.

It sounded almost like a fairy tale.

About the Author

Wendy Loggia has written several novels for young adults. She and her prince are living happily ever after in their New Jersey castle.